The Rover Boys On Treasure Isle or The Strange Cruise of the Steam Yacht.

by

Arthur M. Winfield
(Edward Stratemeyer)

The Rover Boys On Treasure Isle
or The Strange Cruise of the Steam Yacht.
by Arthur M. Winfield
(Edward Stratemeyer)

Copyright © 2024

All Rights reserved.
No part of this publication may be reproduced, stored in a retrieval system, or transmitted in any form or by any means, electronic, mechanical, photocopying or Otherwise, without the written permission of the publisher.

The author/editor asserts the moral right to be identified as the author/editor of this work.

ISBN: 978-93-57273-41-1

Published by
DOUBLE 9 BOOKS
2/13-B, Ansari Road
Daryaganj, New Delhi – 110002
info@double9books.com
www.double9books.com
Tel. 011-40042856

This book is under public domain

ABOUT THE AUTHOR

Arthur M. Winfield (Edward Stratemeyer) was born on October 4, 1862, to Henry Julius Stratemeyer a tobacconist, and Anna Siegel. He was an American publisher, writer of Children's fiction, and founder of the Stratemeyer Syndicate. He was probably the most creative author in the world, producing over 1,300 books and selling over 500 million copies. He also created many famous fictional book series for juveniles, including The Rover boys, The Bobbsey Twins, Tom Swift, The Hardy boys, and Nancy Drew. As a teenager, Stratemeyer worked at his own printing press in the basement of his father's tobacco shop, distributing flyers and brochures to his relatives. These included stories titled The Newsboys Adventure and The Tale of a Lumberman. After graduating from high school, he worked in his father's shop. He is not even 26 in 1888 while Stratemeyer sold his first story Victor Horton's Idea, to the famous children magazine The Golden Days.

CONTENTS

INTRODUCTION 7

CHAPTER I.
BOUND FOR HOME 8

CHAPTER II.
AN IMPORTANT TELEGRAM 14

CHAPTER III.
FUN ON THE FARM 19

CHAPTER IV.
A MIDNIGHT SEARCH 25

CHAPTER V.
AT THE OLD MILL 31

CHAPTER VI.
THE STORY OF A TREASURE 37

CHAPTER VII.
IN WHICH SOMETHING IS MISSING 43

CHAPTER VIII.
THE ROVER BOYS IN NEW YORK 49

CHAPTER IX.
A CHASE ON THE BOWERY 55

CHAPTER X.
DICK BECOMES A PRISONER 61

CHAPTER XI.
ABOARD THE STEAM YACHT 67

CHAPTER XII.
SOMETHING ABOUT FIRECRACKERS 73

CHAPTER XIII.
A WILD AUTOMOBILE RIDE 79

CHAPTER XIV.
WHAT A ROMAN CANDLE DID 85

CHAPTER XV.
THE SAILING OF THE STEAM YACHT 91

CHAPTER XVI.
A ROW ON SHIPBOARD 97

CHAPTER XVII.
A MISHAP IN THE FOG 103

CHAPTER XVIII.
THE NEW DECK HAND 109

CHAPTER XIX.
TREASURE ISLE AT LAST 115

CHAPTER XX.
THE BOYS MAKE A DISCOVERY 121

CHAPTER XXI.
SCARING OFF THE ENEMY 127

CHAPTER XXII.
PRISONERS IN THE FOREST 133

CHAPTER XXIII.
WHAT WINGATE HAD TO TELL 139

CHAPTER XXIV.
A MISSING LANDMARK 144

CHAPTER XXV.
THE TRAIL THROUGH THE JUNGLE 149

CHAPTER XXVI.
A DISMAYING DISCOVERY 154

CHAPTER XXVII.
WHAT HAPPENED ON THE STEAM YACHT 159

CHAPTER XXVIII.
A NEW MOVE OF THE ENEMY 164

CHAPTER XXIX.
THE HUNT FOR THE TREASURE 169

CHAPTER XXX.
HOMEWARD BOUND—CONCLUSION 175

INTRODUCTION.

My DEAR Boys: This is a complete tale in itself, but forms the thirteenth volume of the "Rover Boys Series for Young Americans."

This line of books was started some ten years ago with the publication of the first three volumes, "The Rover Boys at School …
.. The Rover Boys on the Ocean" and "The Rover Boys in the Jungle." At that time I thought to end the series with a fourth volume provided the readers wanted another. But with the publication of "The Rover Boys Out West," came a cry for "more!" and so I added "On the Great Lakes," "In the Mountains," "In Camp," "On Land and Sea," "On the River," "On the Plains," "In Southern Waters" and "On the Farm," where we last left our friends.

For a number of years Tom, Dick and Sam have attended a military academy, but now their school days at Putnam Hall are at an end, and we find them getting ready to go to college. But before leaving home for the higher seat of learning they take a remarkable cruise on a steam yacht, searching for an island upon which it is said a large treasure is hidden. They are accompanied on this trip by their father and a number of friends, and have several adventures somewhat out of the ordinary, and also a good bit of fun for there is bound to be fun when Tom Rover is around. They lose themselves and lose their yacht, and once some of them come pretty close to losing their lives, but in the end—well, the story will tell the rest.

I cannot close without again thanking my many friends for all the nice things they have said about the "Rover Boys" stories and the "Putnam Hall" stories. I trust the present volume will fulfill every fair expectation.

Affectionately and sincerely yours,

EDWARD STRATEMEYER

CHAPTER I.
BOUND FOR HOME

"HURRY Up, Sam, unless you want to be left behind!"

"I'm coming!" shouted Sam Rover, as he crossed the depot platform on the run. "Where is Tom?"

"He went ahead, to get two good seats for us," answered Dick Rover. He looked around the crowd that had gathered to take the train. "Hi, there, Songbird, this way! Come in this car, Hans!"

"Say, aren't you fellows coming aboard?" came a voice from the nearest car, and a curlytopped head with a pair of laughing eyes appeared. "Folks crowding in to beat the band! Come on in if you want seats."

"We'll be in directly," answered Sam, and followed his brother Dick to the car steps. Here there was quite a jam, and the Rover boys had all they could do to get into the car, followed by half a dozen of their school chums. But Tom Rover had managed to keep seats for all, and they sat "in a bunch," much to their satisfaction. Then the train rolled out of the station, and the journey homeward was begun.

The term at Putnam Hall Military Academy was at an end, and the school days of the three Rover boys at that institution were now a thing of the past. Each had graduated with honors, yet all were a trifle sad to think that there would be no going back to a place where they had made so many friends.

"It's almost like giving up your home," Dick had said, several times, while at the actual parting Sam had had to do his best to keep back the tears which welled up in his eyes. Even fun-loving Tom had stopped a good deal of his whistling and had looked unusually sober.

"We'll never have such good times as we've had at Putnam Hall," Sam had said, but he was mistaken, as later events proved.

The three Rover boys did not wish to part from their many school chums, yet they were, more than anxious to get home, and for this there was a very good reason. Their father had told them that he had a very important communication to make to them one regarding how the summer was to be spent. So far no arrangements had been made for the vacation, and the brothers were anxious to know "what was in the wind," as Tom expressed it.

"Maybe we are to prepare for college," said Dick.

"Perhaps we are to go on another trip to Africa?" added Sam.

"Or start on a hunt for the North Pole," put in Tom. "That would be just the thing for this hot weather."

"I can tell you one thing," went on Dick. "Whatever father has on his mind is of a serious nature. It is no mere outing for pleasure."

"I know that," answered Sam, "I could see it by the look on his face."

"Well, we'll know all about it by this time tomorrow," said Tom. "I hope it is some trip—I love to travel," and his brothers nodded their heads in approval.

To those who have read any of the twelve previous volumes in this "Rover Boys Series" the three brothers will need no special introduction. For the benefit of new readers allow me to state that Dick was the oldest, fun-loving Tom next, and Sam the youngest. They were the sons of Anderson Rover, a widower and rich mine owner. The father was a great traveler, and for years the boys had made their home with their uncle, Randolph Rover, and their Aunt Martha, on a farm called Valley Brook, in the heart of New York state.

From the farm, and while their father was in Africa, the boys had been sent to Putnam Hall, as related in the first volume of this series, entitled, "The Rover Boys at School." At the Hall they made a score of friends and several enemies, some of which will be introduced later. A term at school was followed by a trip on the ocean, and then one into the jungles of the Dark Continent in search of Mr. Rover, who had mysteriously disappeared. Then the Rover boys went out west and to the great lakes, and later spent a fine time hunting in the mountains. They likewise spent some time in camp with their fellow cadets, and during the summer vacation took a long trip on land and sea. Then they returned home, and during another vacation sailed down the

Ohio River in a houseboat, spent some time on the plains, took an unexpected trip to southern waters, and then came back to the farm.

On getting back home, as related in the twelfth volume of this series, called "The Rover Boys on the Farm," the boys had imagined that adventures for them were a thing of the past. They were willing to take it easy, but this was not to be. Some bad men, including a sharper named Sid Merrick, were responsible for the theft of some freight from the local railroad, and Merrick, by a slick trick, obtained possession of some traction company bonds belonging to Randolph Rover. The Rover boys managed to locate the freight thieves, but Sid Merrick got away from them, dropping a pocketbook containing the traction company bonds in his flight. This was at a time when Dick, Tom and Sam had returned to Putnam Hall for their final term at that institution. At the Hall they had made a bitter enemy of a big, stocky bully named Tad Sobber and of another lad named Nick Pell. Tad Sobber, to get even with the Rovers for a fancied injury, sent to the latter a box containing a live, poisonous snake. The snake got away and hid in Nick Pell's desk and Nick was bitten and for some time it was feared that he might die. He exposed Tad Sobber, and fearing arrest the bully ran away from the Hall. Later, much to their surprise, the Rover boys learned that the bully was a ward and nephew of Sid Merrick, and when the sharper disappeared, Tad Sobber went with him.

"They are certainly a bad pair," said Dick, but how bad the Rovers were still to find out.

With the boys on the train were John Powell, better known as "Songbird," because he had a, habit of reciting newly made doggerell which he called poetry, Hans Mueller, a German youth who frequently got his English badly twisted, Fred Garrison, who had graduated with the Rovers, and some others.

"Dick, you haven't told me yet what you intended to do this summer," remarked Fred Garrison, as the train rolled on.

"Because I don't know, Fred," answered the elder Rover. "My father has something in store, but I don't know what it is."

"Can't you guess?"

"No."

"I wish we could take another trip like that on the houseboat—it was certainly a dandy."

"The best ever!" put in Tom. "Even if we did have trouble with Lew Flapp, Dan Baxter and some others."

"Speaking of Dan Baxter puts me in mind of something," came from Songbird Powell. "It has just leaked out that Tad Sobber sent a note to Captain Putnam in which Tad blamed some of the cadets for his troubles, and said he was going to get square some day."

"Did he mention any names?" questioned Sam.

"Yes."

"Mine?"

"Yes—and Dick's and Tom's, too."

"It is just like Sobber—to blame his troubles on somebody else," remarked Dick.

"I am not afraid of him," declared Tom. "He had better keep his distance unless he wants to get the worst of it. We used to put up with a whole lot from Dan Baxter before he reformed—I am not going to put up with as much from Sobber."

"Tad certainly went off in bad company," said Sam. "His uncle ought to be in prison this minute."

"Have the authorities heard anything of Merrick?" asked Songbird.

"Not a thing."

"I dink me dot feller has skipped to Europe alretty," vouchsafed Hans Mueller. "He vould peen afraid to stay py der United States in, yah!" And the German boy shook his head wisely.

"Personally I never want to set eyes on Sobber again," said Dick, with a shrug of his broad shoulders. "The idea of introducing that deadly snake into the school was the limit. Why, half a dozen of us might have been bitten instead of only poor Pell."

"Maybe he did it only for a joke," said Larry Colby, another of the cadets.

"If he did, it was carrying a joke altogether too far—endangering one or more human lives. I don't believe in that sort of fun."

"Nor do I," came from several.

"If he is in Europe with his uncle perhaps I'll meet him there," said Larry Colby. "I am going to France and Italy with my uncle and cousin. Wish some of you fellows were going along," he added, wistfully.

"I am going to the Maine woods," said a lad named George Granberry. "You can never guess who is going there, too."

"Who?"

"William Philander Tubbs and Mr. Strong."

"What, our own dude going to camp in the wilderness," cried Tom. "Oh, if I was only along wouldn't I give him some surprises!"

"I'll have some fun don't forget that!" replied George, with a grin. "But as Mr. Strong is going to be along, of course I'll have to be a little careful."

"Dear Mr. Strong!" murmured Sam, with a sigh. "What a fine teacher he is, and how I hate to give him up!"

"I envy your having him along," said Dick.

At that moment the train rolled into a station and Larry and some of the others got off.

"We leave you at the next station," said Songbird, to the Rovers. "When you find out what you are going to do this summer, write and let me know."

"I certainly shall," answered Dick.

The three Rover boys soon after found themselves alone. They had to make a change of cars, and some time later rolled into the station at Oak Run.

"Home again!" shouted Tom, as he alighted on the depot platform.

"Yes, and there is Uncle Randolph waiting for us," added Dick, as he hurried forward to meet his relative. "How do you do, Uncle!" he cried.

"I am well, Richard," answered Randolph Rover, and then he shook hands with all three boys. "Your—er—your father—" he began and hesitated.

"Father? What of him?" asked Tom, in quick alarm, for he saw that his uncle was much disturbed.

"Isn't he with you?"

"Why, no!" answered the three, in a chorus.

"He started for home last night," added Dick.

"Took the train after the one you and Aunt Martha took."

"But he didn't come home," said Randolph Rover.

"Didn't come home?"

"No."

"Didn't he send any word?" questioned Sam.

"None that I received."

"He said he was going straight home would telephone from Lockville for the carriage to meet the last train," said Tom. "This is mighty queer."

It was queer and for the moment the Rover boys and their uncle stared blankly at one another.

"Something is wrong," declared Dick, presently. "And I am going to make it my business to find out at once what it is."

CHAPTER II.
AN IMPORTANT TELEGRAM

Dick Rover would not have been so much disturbed by his father's disappearance had it not been for one thing, which was that Mr. Rover, on leaving the closing exercises at Putnam Hall, had declared that he would take the last train home that night. This train got into Oak Run at one o'clock in the morning, when the station was closed and the platform usually deserted.

"Let us ask around and see if anybody was here when the train came in," suggested Tom.

They first appealed to Mr. Ricks, the station master, an old and crabbed individual, who disliked the boys for the jokes they had played on him in times past. He shook his head at once.

"Don't keep the station open that long," he grunted. "I was home an' in bed, an' I don't know anything about your father."

"Was anybody around the station, that you know of?" went on Dick.

"No."

"Did any telegram come in for our family?"

"If it did I reckon Jackson would send it over, or telephone."

"Let us ask Jackson and make sure," said Sam, and led the way to the telegraph office. The telegraph receiver was ticking away at a lively rate, and Jackson, who had charge of the office, was taking down a message on a blank.

"Hullo!" cried the telegrapher, as he finished and looked up. "Here is a message for Mr. Randolph Rover hot off the wire. It won't take long to deliver it," and he handed it over. "It's paid for," he added. "But you'll have to sign for it," and Mr. Rover did so.

Eagerly all the Rovers read the communication, which ran as follows:

"Am following man I want to catch if possible. May be away from home several days or a week. Very important to see man—trip this summer depends upon it.

"ANDERSON ROVER."

"Wonder who the man can be?" mused Dick, after reading the message twice.

"He has something to do with this matter father was going to tell us about," returned Sam. "It's certainly a mystery."

"Well, this relieves our anxiety," said Randolph Rover. "So long as I know nothing has happened, your father can stay away as long as, he pleases."

"But I am dying to know what it is all about," burst out Tom, who was always impatient to get at the bottom of things. "Uncle Randolph, do you know what father has in mind to do this summer?"

"He talks about taking a sea trip, but where to I don't know."

"And he wants us to go along?" queried the youngest Rover.

"I believe so, Samuel."

"Hurrah! I'd like a sea trip first rate."

"Yes, but—" Mr. Rover lowered his voice. "He doesn't want anybody to know where to. It's some kind of a secret—very important, I imagine—something to do with a gold mine, or something of the sort. He did not give me any particulars."

"He said he was going to let us know about it when we got home from the Hall," said Dick. "I hope he catches his man."

"Wonder who it can be?" came from Tom.

Nobody could answer that question, and in a thoughtful mood the three Rover boys followed their uncle to the carriage and got in. Then the team was touched up and away they whirled, out of the village, across Swift River, and in the direction of Valley Brook farm.

It was a beautiful day in June and never had the country looked finer. As they swept along the well kept road Dick drew a deep breath of satisfaction.

"This air makes a fellow feel new all over!" he declared.

"I suppose you are going to plant and grow some wonderful things this summer, Uncle Randolph," said Tom. His uncle had studied scientific farming for years, but had never made any tremendous success of it in fact his experiments usually cost him considerably more than they brought in.

"Well—er—I am trying my hand this year on some Mexican melons said to be very fine, Thomas," was the reply.

"Mexican melons?" said the fun-loving Tom, innocently. "That puts me in mind when I was over to Albany last I saw a pumpkin in a restaurant window eight feet high and at least ten feet across."

"Is it possible!" ejaculated Randolph Rover, gazing at his nephew incredulously.

"Sure thing. The pumpkin looked to be good, too. They had a lot of pumpkin pies set around it, just for an advertisement."

"Thomas, did you measure that pumpkin?"

"No; why should I?"

"Then how do you know it was eight feet high and ten feet across?"

"Why, Uncle Randolph, I didn't say the pumpkin was eight feet high and ten feet across. I said I saw it in a restaurant window eight feet high and ten feet across," and Tom drew down the corners of his mouth soberly.

"Tom, that's the worst ever!" cried Sam.

"You ought to be made to walk home for that," added Dick.

"Thomas! Thomas! you are as bad as ever!" said Mr. Rover, with a sigh. "But I might have been on my guard. I know there are no pumpkins of that size."

"Uncle Randolph, you'll have to forgive me," said Tom, putting his hand affectionately on his relative's shoulder. "I really couldn't help it—I am just bubbling over to think that school days are over and I won't have to do any studying for several months to come."

"I fancy we'll have to tie you down to keep you out of mischief."

"You won't have to tie me down if I go on a sea trip with dad."

"Haven't you had sea trips enough with being cast away in the middle of the Pacific, and being wrecked in the Gulf of Mexico? It seems to me every time you and the others leave home something serious happens to you."

"True but we always come back right side up with care and all charges paid," answered the fun-loving Rover airily.

They soon made a turn in the road which brought them in sight of the big farmhouse, nestling comfortably in a group of stately trees. As they turned into the lane their Aunt Martha came to the front piazza and waved her hand. Down in the roadway stood Jack Ness; the hired man, grinning broadly, and behind Mrs. Rover stood Alexander Pop, the colored helper, his mouth open from ear to ear. At once Tom began to sing:

"Home again! home again! Safe from Putnam Hall."

And then he made a flying leap from the carriage, rushed up the steps and gave his aunt such a hug as made her gasp for breath.

"Oh, Tom, you bear! Do let up!" she cried. "Now, there's a kiss for you, and there's another! How do you do, Sam, and how are you, Dick?" And she kissed them also. "I am glad you are back at last." She turned to her husband "What of Anderson, did you hear anything?"

"Yes, he will be back in a few days."

"I'se jess too pleased fo' anything to see yo' boys back heah!" came from Aleck Pop. "It's dun been mighty lonely since yo' went away."

"Don't worry, Aleck, we'll cheer you up," answered Tom.

"Oh, I know dat, Massa Tom yo'll turn dis place upside down in two days suah!"

"Why, Aleck, you know I'd never do anything so rash," answered Tom, meekly.

"Going to uncover some more freight thieves?" asked Jack Ness, as he took charge of the team and started for the barn.

"I think dem boys had bettah cotch some of dem chicken thieves," put in Aleck Pop. "Yo' don't seem to git holt ob dem nohow."

"Oh, never you mind about the chicken thieves," grumbled Jack Ness.

"Has somebody been stealing chickens again?" asked Dick, remembering that they had suffered several times from such depradations.

"Yes, da has took two chickens las' Wednesday, foah on Saturday, an' two on Monday. Jack he laid fo' 'em wid a shotgun, but he didn't cotch nobody."

"I'll catch them yet, see if I don't," said the hired man.

"Perhaps a fox is doing it," suggested Sam. "If so, we ought to go on a fox hunt. That would suit me first rate."

"No fox in this," answered Jack Ness. "I see the footprints of two men,—tramps, I reckon. If I catch sight of 'em I'll fill 'em full of shot and then have 'em locked up."

CHAPTER III.
FUN ON THE FARM

Two days passed and the boys felt once more at home on the farm. The strain of the recent examinations and the closing exercises at school had gone and as Sam declared, "they were once more themselves," and ready for anything that might turn up.

In those two days came another telegram from Mr. Rover, sent from Philadelphia, in which he stated that he had caught his man, but had lost him again. He added that he would be home probably on the following Sunday. This message came in on Monday, so the boys knew they would have to wait nearly a week before seeing their parent.

"I am just dying to know what it is all about," said Tom, and the others said practically the same.

Tom could not keep down his propensities for joking and nearly drove Sarah, the cook, to distraction by putting some barn mice in the bread box in the pantry and by pouring ink over some small stones and then adding them to the coal she was using in the kitchen range. He also took a piece of old rubber bicycle tire and trimmed it up to resemble a snake and put it in Jack Ness' bed in the barn, thereby nearly scaring the hired man into a fit. Ness ran out of the room in his night dress and raised such a yell that he aroused everybody in the house. He got his shotgun and blazed away at the supposed snake, thereby ruining a blanket, two sheets, and filling the mattress with shot. When he found out how he had been hoaxed he was the most foolish looking man to be imagined.

"You just wait, Master Tom, I'll get square," he said.

"Who said I put a snake in your bed?" demanded Tom. "I never did such a thing in my life."

"No, but you put that old rubber in, and I know it," grumbled the hired man and then went back to bed.

Tom also had his little joke on Aleck Pop. One evening he saw the colored man dressing up to go out and learned that he was going to call on a colored widow living at Dexter's Corners, a nearby village.

"We can't allow this," said the fun-loving Rover to his younger brother. "The next thing you know Aleck will be getting married and leaving us."

"What do you think of doing?" asked Sam.

"Come on, and I'll show you."

Now, Aleck was rather a good looking and well formed darkey and he was proud of his shape. He had a fine black coat, with trousers to match, and a gorgeous colored vest. This suit Tom was certain he would wear when calling on the widow.

When in Ithaca on his way home the fun-loving Rover had purchased an imitation rabbit, made of thin rubber. This rabbit had a small rubber hose attached, and by blowing into the hose the rabbit could be blown up to life size or larger.

Leading the way to Aleck's room, Tom got out the colored man's coat and placed the rubber rabbit in the middle of the back, between the cloth and the lining. It was put in flat and the hose was allowed to dangle down under the lining to within an inch of the split of the coat tails, and at this point Tom put a hole in the lining, so he could get at the end of the hose with ease.

It was not long before Aleck came in to dress. It was late and he was in a hurry, for he knew he had a rival, a man named Jim Johnson, and he did not want Johnson to get to the widow's home ahead of him. He washed up and donned his clothing with rapidity, and never noticed that anything was wrong with the coat.

"Now, Sam, you fix his necktie for him," whispered Tom, who, with his younger brother, was lying in wait outside the house. "Tell him it doesn't set just straight."

Sam understood, and as soon as Aleck appeared he sauntered up side by side with Tom.

"Hullo, Aleck, going to see your best girl?" he said pleasantly.

"I'se gwine to make a little call, dat's all."

"He's after the widow Taylor," put in Tom. "He knows she's got ten thousand or so in the bank."

"Massa Tom, you dun quit yo' foolin'," expostulated Aleck.

"If you are going to make a society call you want your necktie on straight," said Sam. "It's a fine tie, but it's no good the way you have it tied. Here, let me fix it," and he pulled the tie loose.

"I did hab a lot ob trubble wid dat tie," agreed the colored man.

"It's too far around," went on Sam, and gave the tie a jerk, first one way and another. Then he began to tie it, shoving Aleck again as he did so.

In the meantime Tom had gotten behind the colored man and was blowing up the rubber rabbit. As the rubber expanded Aleck's coat went up with it, until it looked as if the man was humpbacked. Then Tom fastened the hose, so the wind could not get out of it. Next the youth brought out a bit of chalk and in big letters wrote on the black coat as follows:

I have got to
HUMP
to catch the
widow.

"Now your tie is something like,"
declared Sam, after a wink from Tom.
"It outshines everything I ever saw."

"I'se got to be a going," answered Aleck. "Much obliged."

"Now, Aleck, hump yourself and you'll get the widow sure along with her fourteen children."

"She ain't got but two children," returned the colored man, and hurried away. His appearance, with the hump on his back and the sign, caused both the Rovers to burst out laughing.

"Come on, I've got to see the end of this," said Tom, and led the way by a side path to the Widow Taylor's cottage. This was a short cut, but Aleck would not take it, because of the briar bushes and the dust. As the boys were in their knockaround suits they did not mind this.

The widow's cottage was a tumbled down affair on a side street of Dexter's Corners. A stovepipe stuck out of a back window, and the front door lacked the lower hinge. In the front yard the weeds were several feet high.

"I don't see why Aleck wants to come and see such a person as this," observed Sam. "She may be pretty, as colored widows go, but she is certainly lazy and shiftless."

"Yes, and she has more than two children and I know it. Why, once I came past here and I saw her with at least seven or eight."

When the boys came up they saw several colored children hurrying away from the house. As they did this the widow came to the door and called after them:

"Now, Arabella, go to the cemetery, jest as I tole yo', an' stay thar!"

"I ain't gwine to stay long," answered Arabella.

"You stay an hour or two," answered the widow. "To morrow, I'll give yo' money fer lolly pops."

"What is she sending the children to the cemetery for?" asked Tom, in a whisper.

"Maybe to keep 'em quiet," answered Sam, with a grin.

"Must be wanting to keep them out of Aleck's way."

At that moment the figure of a tall, lanky colored man came down a side street. The man entered the widow's cottage and received a warm welcome.

"Glad to see you, Mistah Thomas. Hopes yo' is feelin' fine this ebenin'," said the widow graciously.

"I'se come fo' to make yo' an offah," said Mr. Thomas. "Yo' said yo' would mahrry me soon as I had a job. Well, I'se got de job now."

"Is it a steady job?"

"Yes, at de stone quarry dribin' a stone wagon."

"How much yo' gits a week, Peter?"

"Twelve dollahs," was the proud answer.

"Den I closes wid you," said the widow, and allowed the suitor to embrace her.

Just then Aleck came in sight. As he saw the couple through the open door he straightened up.

"Maybe yo' didn't look fo' me around, Mrs. Taylor," he said, stiffly.

"Oh, Yes, I did, Mistah Pop," she said, sweetly. "But yo' see—I—dat is—" She stopped short. "Wot's dat?" she cried.

"Wot?"

"Dat hump on yo' back?"

"Ain't no hump on my back," answered Aleck.

"Suah da is."

"He's got a sign on, too," put in Peter Thomas. "Look wot it reads, 'I hab got to hump to cotch de widow.' Hah! hah! hah! Dot's a good one."

"Yo' needn't hump yo'self to cotch me," cried the widow, wrathfully. "I'se engaged to Mistah Thomas." And she smiled on the individual in question.

Crestfallen and bewildered, Aleck felt of his back and took off his coat. He squeezed the rubber rabbit so hard that it exploded with a bang, scaring himself and the others.

"Dat's a trick on me!" roared the Rover's man, and tore the rabbit from his coat. "Dem boys did dat!"

"I can't see yo' to night, or any udder night, Mistah Pop," said the widow. "I'se engaged to Mistah Thomas."

"Den good night," growled Aleck, and turning on his heel he started for home.

Tom and Sam saw that he was angry, yet they had to roar at the scene presented. They wondered what Aleck would say when he got back to the farm.

"We have got to square ourselves," said Tom.

"How are you going to do it?"

"Oh, we'll do it somehow."

They took the short cut, but so did Aleck, and consequently all three soon met.

"Yo' played dat joke yo' can't go fo' to deny it!" cried the colored man.

"We are not going to deny it, Aleck," said Tom. "But it was no joke. We did it for your good."

"Huh!"

"We certainly did," put in Sam. "Why, Aleck, we can't bear to think of your getting married and leaving us."

"Huh!"

"We want you to stay with us," said Tom. "Besides, that widow has a lot of children and is after your money."

"She ain't got but two chillen. She had moah, but she dun told me all but two was in de seminary."

"The seminary?" queried Tom. Then a light broke in on him. "You mean the cemetery."

"Persackly—de place da puts de dead folks."

"Well, they are in the cemetery right enough—but they are a long way from being dead."

"Wot yo' mean, Tom?"

"We saw her send five of them away this evening—she told 'em to go to the cemetery and stay there awhile."

"Wot! Yo' is fooling dis chile!"

"It is absolutely true," said Sam. "I am quite sure she has seven children."

"Huh! If dat's de case dat Thomas nigger can hab her," grumbled Aleck, and walked on. "But I ain't takin' yo' word fo' dis," he added cautiously. "I'se gwine to make a few investigations to morrow."

"Do so—and you'll thank us from the bottom of your heart," answered Tom; and there the subject was dropped. It may be added here that later on Aleck discovered that the widow had ten children and was head over heels in debt, and he was more than glad that the boys had played the trick on him, and that the other colored man had gained Mrs. Taylor's hand.

CHAPTER IV.
A MIDNIGHT SEARCH

That night was destined to be an eventful one on the Rover farm. Arriving home, Sam and Tom told of the fun they had had and Dick laughed heartily. Then all three of the boys went to bed.

About midnight came a loud shouting from the barn, followed by the report of a shotgun. This was followed by a shriek from Sarah, the cook, who was afraid that burglars had come to murder her.

"What's that?" questioned Dick, as he hopped out of bed.

"That's Jack Ness' gun," answered Tom. "Something must be wrong at the barn."

"Chicken thieves again—I'll bet a new hat," said Sam.

By this time Randolph Rover and his wife were up and were lighting a lamp. Without waiting for them, the boys slipped on some clothing and their shoes and ran downstairs. Dick took with him a pistol and each of the others a baseball bat.

"Boys! boys! be careful!" shouted their uncle after them.

"All right," returned Dick, readily.

He was the first outside, but Sam and Tom were close upon his heels. He heard Jack Ness running to the edge of a cornfield, shouting lustily. Then came another report of the shotgun.

"What is it, Jack?" shouted Dick. "Who are you shooting at?"

"I'm after two men," was the hired man's reply. "They jest run into the cornfield."

"Chicken thieves?" queried Tom.

"I guess so—anyway they was prowlin' around the hen house an' the barn. I called an' asked 'em what they wanted and they ran for dear life—so I knew they was up to no good."

"They certainly must have been chicken thieves, or worse," was Sam's comment. "Really, this is getting to be too much," he added. "We ought to catch them and have them locked up."

"I'm willing to go after them," answered Tom, readily.

"Did you get a good look at the rascals?" asked Dick.

"Not very good," answered Jack Ness.

"They weren't boys, were they?"

"No—they were men—both tall and heavy fellows."

"Did you ever see them before?" asked Tom. "Not that I can remember."

While they were talking the party of four had run down to the edge of the cornfield. This spot was really a peach orchard, but the trees were still so small that the ground was being utilized that season for corn, planted in rows between the trees. The corn was not yet full grown, but it was high enough to conceal a man lying flat or crouching down.

The sky was filled with stars and the old moon was beginning to show over the hills beyond the valley, so it was fairly light across the field. The boys kept their eyes on the corn and the peach trees, but failed to discover any persons moving among them.

"My shotgun is empty—maybe I had better go back and load up," said the hired man.

"Yes, do it, but hurry up," answered Dick. "I'll stay here on guard with the pistol."

The hired man ran off toward the barn.
Hardly had he disappeared when
Sam gave a short cry and pointed into the field
with his hand.

"I saw somebody raise up just now and look around," he said. "He is out of sight now."

"Where?" came from Dick and Tom quickly. "Over yonder by the twisted peach tree."

"I'll investigate," said Dick. "You can come along if you want to. Keep your eyes open for both men. We don't want either to get away if we can help it."

The three lads spread out in something of a semi circle and advanced slowly into the field, keeping their eyes and ears on the alert for anything out of the ordinary. Thus they covered fifty yards, when Tom found himself near one of the largest of the peach trees. As he passed this a form arose quickly from under a bough, caught him by the waist and threw him forcibly to the ground.

"Hi!" yelled Tom. "Let up!" And then he made a clutch for his assailant, catching him by the foot. But the man broke away and went crashing through the corn, calling on "Shelley" to follow him.

The yell from Tom attracted the attention of Dick and Sam, and they turned to learn what had happened to their brother. As they did this a second man leaped up from the corn in front of them and started to run in the direction of the river.

"Stop!" called out Dick. "Stop, or I'll fire on you!" And then he discharged his pistol into the air as a warning. The man promptly dodged behind a row of peach trees, but kept on running as hard as ever.

The Rover boys were now thoroughly aroused, and all three started in pursuit of the two men. They saw the fellows leave the field and hurry down a lane leading to Swift River.

"I believe they are going to the river. Maybe they have a boat," said Tom.

"I shouldn't wonder," answered Dick.

"I wish they would take to a boat," said Sam. "We could follow them easily—in Dan Bailey's boat."

"Hi, where are you?" came a shout from behind, and they saw Jack Ness returning. "Your uncle and aunt want you to be careful—they are afraid those villains will shoot you."

"We'll be careful," answered Tom. "But we are going to capture them if it can be done," he added, sturdily.

The hired man had reloaded the shotgun and also brought some additional ammunition with him. He was nervous and the boys could readily see that he did not relish continuing the pursuit.

"We can't do nothin' in the dark," he grumbled. "Let us wait till morning."

"No, I am going after them now," answered Dick, decidedly.

"So am I," added Sam and Tom.

They were going forward as rapidly as the semi darkness would permit. The ground was more or less uncertain, and once the youngest Rover went into a mud hole, splashing the mud up into Jack Ness' face.

"Hi, stop that!" spluttered the hired man. "Want to put my eye out?"

"Excuse me, Jack, I didn't see the hole," answered Sam.

"It ain't safe to walk here in the dark—somebody might break a leg."

"If you want to go back you can do so," put in Dick. "Give Tom the shotgun."

"Oh—er—I'm goin' if you be," answered Jack Ness. He was ashamed to let them know how much of a coward he really was.

It was quite a distance to Swift River, which at this point ran among a number of stately willows. As the boys gained the water's edge they saw a boat putting out not a hundred feet away.

"There they are!" cried Dick.

"Stop!" yelled Tom. "Stop, unless you want to be shot!"

"We'll do a little shooting ourselves if you are not careful!" came back in a harsh voice.

"Take care! Take care!" cried Jack Ness, in terror, and ran to hide behind a handy tree.

The two men in the boat were putting down the stream with all speed. The current, always strong, soon carried them around a bend and out of sight.

It must be confessed that the boys were in a quandary. They did not wish to give up the chase, yet they realized that the escaping men might be desperate characters and ready to put up a hard fight if cornered.

"Jack, I think you had better run over to the Ditwold house and tell them what is up," said Dick, after a moment's thought. "Tell Ike and Joe we are going to follow in Dan Bailey's boat." The Ditwolds were neighboring farmers and Ike and Joe were strong young men ever ready to lend a hand in time of trouble.

"All right," answered the hired man, and set off, first, however, turning his firearm over to Tom.

The three Rover boys were well acquainted with the river, and had had more than one adventure on its swiftly flowing waters, as my old readers know. They skirted a number of the willows and came to a small creek, where they found Dan Bailey's craft tied to a stake. But there were no oars, and they gazed at one another in dismay.

"We might have known it," said Dick, in disgust. "He always takes the oars up to the barn with him."

The barn was a good distance off and none of the boys relished running that far for oars. More than this, they felt that by the time the oars were brought the other craft would be out of sight and hearing, and thus the trail of the midnight prowlers would be lost.

"Here is a bit of board," said Sam, searching around. "Let us use that for a paddle. The current will carry us almost as swiftly as if we were rowing. The main thing will be to keep out of the way of the rocks."

"I wish those chaps would run on the rocks and smash their boat to bits," grumbled Tom, who had gotten a stone in his loose shoe and was consequently limping.

The boys shoved the rowboat from the creek to the river and leaped in. Dick, being the largest and strongest, took the board and using it as a sweep, sent the craft well out where the current could catch it. Down the stream went the boat, with Sam in the middle and Tom in the stern. There was no rudder, so they had to depend entirely upon Dick, who stood up near the bow, peering ahead for rocks, of which the river boasted a great number.

"Those fellows must know this river," remarked Sam, as he started to lace his shoes, there being nothing else just then to do.

"They ought to—if they are the fellows who visited our henhouse before," answered Tom. "Dick, can you see them?"

"No, but I know they must be ahead."

"Perhaps they went ashore—just to fool us."

"They couldn't get ashore here very well—it is too rocky, you know that as well as I do. Listen!"

They listened, but the only sound that broke the stillness was the distant roar of Humpback Falls, where Sam had once had such a thrilling adventure, as related in "The Rover Boys at School." Even now, so long afterward, it made the youngest Rover shiver to think of that happening.

A minute later the boat came clear of the tree shadows and the boys saw a long stretch ahead of them, shimmering like silver in the moonbeams. Sam, looking in the direction of the opposite shore, made out a rowboat moving thither.

"There they are!" he cried.

At once Dick essayed to turn their own craft in that direction. But with only a bit of a board for a paddle, and with the current tearing along wildly, this was not easy. The rowboat was turned partly, but then scraped some rocks, and they were in dire peril of upsetting.

"I see where they are going!" cried Tom. "To the old Henderson mill."

"We'll have to land below that point," said his oldest brother. "If I try to get in there with only this board I'll hit the rocks sure."

"They are taking chances, even with oars," was Sam's comment. "See, they have struck some rocks!"

He was right, and the Rovers saw the boat ahead spin around and the two men leap to their feet in alarm. But then the craft steadied itself, and a moment later shot into the shadows of the trees beside the old flour mill.

It was not until five minutes later that Dick was able to guide their own rowboat to the shore upon which the mill was located. They hit several rocks, but at last came in where there was a sandy stretch. All leaped out, and the craft was hauled up to a point out of the current's reach.

"Now to get back to the mill as soon as possible, and corner those fellows if we can," said Tom, and without delay the three Rover boys started through the woods in the direction of the spot where the two men had landed.

CHAPTER V.
AT THE OLD MILL

The Henderson mill was now largely so only in name. So far back as the Rover boys could remember, it had been a tenantless structure going slowly to decay. The water wheel was gone, and so were the grinding stones, and the roof and sides were full of holes. Henderson, the owner, had years ago fallen heir to a fortune, and had moved away, leaving the building at the mercy of the tramps who frequently stopped there.

It was no easy matter to climb around or over the rocks which lay between the boys and the old mill, and the darkness under the thick trees was intense. They felt their way along slowly, and Tom was careful to carry the shotgun with the barrel pointed downward, that there might be no accident.

"More than likely those fellows have been putting up at the old mill," said Dick.

"They'll leave now—if they think we are coming," answered Sam.

"Let us keep quiet," put in Tom. "If they hear us talking they will surely skip out."

After that but little was said. Foot by foot they drew closer to the dilapidated structure, until it loomed up dimly before them. Then Dick motioned for the others to halt.

With bated breath the boys listened. At first they heard little but the rushing of the water over the rocks. Then came a sudden cracking of a rotten floor board, followed by an exclamation.

"Confound the luck! I've put my foot through the floor again," growled a man's voice. "Shelley, why don't you light the lantern? Do you want me to break my neck?"

"If I light the lantern the Rovers may come here," was the answer from the man called Shelley.

"Oh, they went down the river I saw them."

"They may have turned in nearby."

Some more words followed, but spoken so low that the boys could not understand them. They heard a faint creaking of the flooring of the old mill, but that was all.

"They are there, that's certain," whispered Dick. "But I don't see how we are going to capture them in this darkness."

"I wish we had a lantern," said the youngest Rover.

"We wouldn't dare to light it, Sam," answered Tom. "Let us crawl up close to the building. Maybe we can find out something more about the men. They may be some good for nothing fellows from the village."

As there seemed nothing else to do, this advice was followed, and soon the boys were at one of the broken out windows of the mill. They listened and looked inside, but saw and heard nothing.

"They are not here," whispered Sam, disappointedly.

"They are not far off," answered his big brother confidently.

"Look!" came from Tom. "A light!"

He pointed through the window to the flooring inside. From between the loose boards shone several streaks of light. As the boys gazed the light vanished and all was as dark as before.

"They are in the lower room, the one where the water wheel used to be," whispered Tom. "Maybe that is where they have been hanging out."

"Come after me—but don't make any noise," said Dick, cautiously. "If they have gone into the second room down there maybe we can make them prisoners!"

"That's the idea!" cried Sam. "Just the thing!"

"Hush, Sam, or you'll spoil all."

Scarcely daring to breathe, now that they knew the strange men were so close, the three Rover boys walked to the open doorway of the old mill and went inside. Dick led the way and crossed to where an enclosed stairs ran to the floor below. On tiptoes he went down, not trusting a step until he was sure of his footing. It was well he did this, for two of the steps were entirely rotted away, and he had to warn his brothers, otherwise one or another might have had a fall.

Standing in the wheel room of the old mill the boys saw another streak of light, coming from the room which Dick had suggested. The door to this was closed, a bolt on the inner side holding it in place. There was another bolt on the outside, which Dick remembered having seen on a previous visit.

"We can lock them in if we wish," he whispered.

"Do it," answered his brothers promptly.

The bolt was large and old fashioned, and Dick had considerable trouble in moving it into its socket. It made a rasping sound, but this was not noticed by the two men, who were conversing earnestly.

"Well, we made a mess of it," growled the man called Shelley.

"So we did. But I didn't think that hired man would wake up. Neither of us made a bit of noise. He must be a light sleeper."

"I only hope they think we were after chickens, Cuffer. If they knew the truth—" The man named Shelley broke off with a coarse laugh.

"Well, we got chickens the other night, didn't we?" and now the man called Cuffer laughed also. "But say, this is getting serious," he went on presently. "Merrick expects us to do this job for him and do it quick, and he won't like it at all when he finds out how we have missed it."

"We can't do the impossible. Those Rovers are too wide awake for us."

"They certainly were too wide awake for Merrick in that traction company bond matter. He was a chump not to sell those bonds as soon as he got hold of them."

"He didn't dare—he was afraid the market was being watched."

"What does he want of those papers, anyway?"

"I don't know exactly. But you know what he said—there would be a small fortune in it for us if we got 'em. He says he's got some papers —or a map I guess it is—but he wants these papers, too. He didn't dare show himself around here—you know the reason why."

"Sure—those Rovers would recognize him, even if he tried to disguise himself."

Dick, Tom and Sam listened to this conversation with keenest interest and amazement. These men had mentioned the name of Sid

Merrick, the rascal who had in the past tried so hard to harm them and who had up to the present time escaped the clutches of the law. Evidently they were in league with Merrick and under his directions.

"We must capture those fellows by all means," whispered Tom, excitedly. "If we do, maybe we can find out where Merrick is."

"Yes, and Tad Sobber, too," added Sam, who had not forgotten the poisonous snake episode at Putnam Hall.

"They weren't after chickens—that was only a blind," said Dick. "They want to get something from the house—some papers that Merrick wants."

"They must be valuable," said Sam.

"Father has all sorts of valuable papers," went on Tom. "Bonds, deeds to mining properties, and such. But I thought he had the most of those in a safe deposit vault in the city."

"So he has," answered Dick. "Maybe these fellows would be fooled even if they got into Uncle Randolph's house. They—Listen!"

Shelley and Cuffer had begun to talk again. They mentioned a tramp steamer called the *Josephine*, and Shelley said she was now in port being repaired. Then the conversation drifted to sporting matters, and Cuffer told how he had lost a hundred dollars on a prize fight.

"That's why I'm here," he added.
"And I want some money the next time
I see Sid Merrick."

"He won't give us any unless we—" said Shelley, and the boys did not hear the end of the sentence, for the speaker tried the door as he spoke, throwing the inner bolt back. Of course with the outer bolt in place, the door refused to budge. The boys drew back, and Tom raised the shotgun and Dick his pistol.

"The door is caught!" cried Shelley, and pushed on it as hard as he could.

"What!" exclaimed Cuffer and leaped forward. He, too, tried to move the barrier. "This is a trick! Somebody has bolted the door on the outside."

"Was there a bolt there?"

"Yes, a heavy one, too."

"Then somebody has trapped us!"

"Open that door!" sang out Cuffer, before his companion could stop him.

"We are not going to open that door," answered Dick, in an equally loud voice. "We have got you fast and we intend to keep you so."

"Who are you?"

"I am Dick Rover, and my two brothers are with me. We are well armed, and we'll shoot if you try to break that door down."

"Caught!" cried Shelley in a rage, and then uttered several exclamations under his breath.

"What are you going to do?" asked Cuffer, after a moment of silence.

"Hold you prisoners until we can get help and then turn you over to the officers of the law."

"We haven't done anything wrong."

"That remains to be seen."

"You haven't any right to lock us in here."

"Then we take the right," answered Tom grimly.

"Let us smash the door down," came in a low tone from inside the room.

"If you try it we'll surely fire," said Dick, and cocked his pistol so the men might hear the click. Tom did the same with the shotgun.

"See here, you let us out and we'll make it all right with you," remarked Shelley, after another pause. "We are not the bad fellows you take us to be. We were only going to play a joke, that's all."

"I suppose you think Sid Merrick's doings are a joke, too," said Sam, before he had time to think twice.

"Ha! what do you know of Merrick?" ejaculated Cuffer. "They must have been listening to our talk," he added, in a low tone to his companion.

"Yes, and if so, we are in a bad box," answered Shelley. "I'd give a good deal to be out of here just now."

"Talk to them, while I take a look around," continued Cuffer, struck by a sudden idea.

Shelley did as told, pleading with the three Rovers to let him go and offering to pay fifty dollars for his liberty. He talked in a loud tone, to cover up what noise his companion might make. The boys listened, but refused to open the door until some sort of help should arrive, or until morning came.

"Sam, you go outside and see if Jack and the Ditwolds are anywhere around," said Dick, and the youngest Rover departed immediately.

Presently Tom and Dick heard Cuffer give a cry of pain.

"You've stepped on my sore toe!" howled the man. "Phew! how it hurts!"

The two men talked about the hurt toe for several minutes. Then their voices suddenly ceased. Tom and Dick strained their ears, but could hear absolutely nothing.

"They must be up to some trick," whispered the eldest Rover. "Hi, you, what are you doing?" he called out.

There was no answer and the silence was just as ominous as before. The light in the inner room had gone out.

"What are you doing?" repeated Dick, and ran close to the door to listen. Nothing but absolute silence followed.

What to do next the two boys did not know. They waited for fully five minutes—then five more. Presently they heard Sam coming back.

"I yelled for Jack and the others, but I got no answer," said he. "What are the men doing?"

"We don't know," answered Tom. "We are afraid they are up to some trick."

"A trick?" repeated Sam. Then he gave a gasp. "The room—isn't there a back door, leading out to the shed?"

"I don't know," answered Dick.

"I'll run and see."

Sam was gone less than two minutes when they heard a cry, and then he pounded on the door they had so carefully guarded.

"There is a back door and it is wide open. The men have gone!" was his dismaying announcement.

CHAPTER VI.
THE STORY OF A TREASURE

It was a disheartening discovery, but the three Rover boys did not stop to think it over. Throwing open the bolted door, Tom and Dick joined Sam, and in the darkness made their way to the rear of the room in which they had held Cuffer and Shelley prisoners. In a minute more they were outside, under the trees at the rear of the old mill.

"Which way did they go?"

Tom asked the question, but nobody could answer it. The moon had now gone under some clouds and it was so dark they could scarcely see ten feet in any direction.

"Perhaps they took to the river again," suggested Sam.

"It is not likely," answered his big brother. "But we can take a look."

They ran around to where the men had landed. Their boat was still in its place, tied to a tree.

"Listen!" cried Sam "Somebody's shouting, and there is a light."

"It is Jack Ness," said Tom.

The boys set up an answering shout, and soon a boat came up to the shore. It contained the hired man and the two Ditwolds. They had a lantern with them and also an old fashioned single barrel shotgun.

The situation was quickly explained, and then the party of six began a systematic search of the woods and the various roads in the vicinity of Henderson's mill. This search lasted until morning, but nothing came of it.

"We may as well give up," said Dick, at last. "They have gotten away and that is all there is to it."

The boys were completely tired out when they got home. Their uncle and aunt were much worried over their prolonged absence and overjoyed to see them return unharmed.

"I was so afraid one of you might get shot or something," said Mrs. Rover. "Some of those, chickens thieves are desperate characters."

"Those men were more than chicken thieves," answered Dick. And he told his uncle and aunt of the conversation overheard at the old mill.

"It is a great pity that they got away," said Randolph Rover.

"What do you imagine they are after, Uncle Randolph?" questioned Sam.

"I do not know, excepting it may be some mining stocks or a deed to some property. Perhaps your father will be able to explain it when he gets back."

The authorities were notified, but they failed to apprehend the men. It was learned that the boat they had used had been stolen from a point near Oak Run, and the craft was returned to its owner. That they had used the old mill for a stopping place was evidenced by the remains of numerous meals found there. The boys made a careful search of the premises, but brought nothing to light which was of use to them.

"I wish father was home—or we knew how to reach him by telephone, or with a telegram," remarked Dick.

"Well, we can't reach him, so we'll have to be patient until he returns," answered Sam. "By the way, I wonder if his going away had anything to do with what those men were up to?"

"It might be so," returned Dick, slowly. "Both happenings are queer, to say the least."

"I wish I knew what father has in mind to do," came from Tom. "I hope we take some kind of a trip. I don't want to stick on the farm all summer."

With nothing to do, the next two days passed slowly. The boys went fishing and swimming, and they also did some shooting at a target which they set up behind the barn, and whiled away, some time at boxing and in gymnastic exercises. Dick also spent an hour in penning a long letter to Dora Stanhope, who, as my old readers are well aware, was his dearest girl friend. Dora and her mother lived not far from Putnam Hall, and Dick and his brothers had become acquainted with her and her two cousins, Nellie and Grace Laning, when they had first gone to school. The Rover boys had on several occasions saved Mrs. Stanhope from serious trouble, and for this the widow was very grateful. She and her daughter had gone with them on the houseboat trip down the Ohio and the Mississippi, and Mrs. Laning and Nellie and Grace had likewise accompanied the party. It may be added here that Tom and Sam thought Nellie and Grace two of the nicest girls in the whole world, which indeed they were.

On Saturday morning the boys were contemplating a bicycle ride when Sam, who chanced to look toward the road, set up a shout:

"Here comes father!"

All gazed in the direction and saw Mr. Rover coming toward them in a rig he had hired at the depot. They ran to meet their parent and were soon shaking him by the hand. They saw that he looked travel worn and tired.

"I have been on the go ever since I left Putnam Hall," said Anderson Rover. "It was a most unexpected trip. I will tell you all about it as soon as I have rested a bit and had something to eat."

"We have something to tell, too," answered Dick. "But that can keep until later."

Inside of an hour Mr. Rover had been served with a good, hot breakfast and then he declared that he felt like a new man. He invited the whole family into the sitting room for a conference of importance.

"I told you lads I had something on my mind," he said. "I did not want to speak of it while at the graduation exercises at the school because there was too much going on. Now I am going to tell you everything and also tell you what I propose to do. But first, I want to listen to what you have to tell me."

It did not take the three boys long to relate the particulars of the pursuit of Cuffer and Shelley, and of what they had overheard at the old mill. Anderson Rover listened with close attention and did not seem surprised when they mentioned Sid Merrick's name.

"That fits in, to a certain degree, with what I have to tell you." he said, when they had finished.

"It is a strange story, and the only way for me to do, so that it will be perfectly clear to you, is to tell it from the beginning."

"Well, we're willing enough to listen," said Dick, with a smile.

"We've been on pins and needles ever since you said you had something important to tell," added Tom, grinning.

"Well, to start, this concerns Mrs. Stanhope more than it concerns ourselves," began the father.

"What!" ejaculated Dick. He had not expected anything of this sort.

"I knew you would be surprised, Dick, and you'll be more surprised when I get through."

"Are the Lanings in this?" questioned Sam, thinking of Grace.

"They are in a certain sense—or will be if everything turns out successfully. When Mr. Stanhope died he left most of his property to Mrs. Stanhope and Dora—the majority to Dora—but a small share was left to the Lanings, they being so closely related and such good friends."

"But what is it all about?" asked Tom, impatiently.

"As I said before, I must start at the beginning, or perhaps you won't understand at all. As you know, Mr. Stanhope died some years ago. He was interested in various business enterprises, including a number of vessels which carried freight between the United States and the West Indies. One of his partners in the freight carrying business was a man named Robertson and another was a Silas Merrick."

"Merrick!" cried Sam.

"Yes, and this Silas Merrick was an older brother to Sid Merrick, the rascal who stole the bonds, and whom you heard mentioned by Cuffer and Shelley. Let me say here that Silas Merrick is dead, and when he died he left all his property to his brother Sidney and his sister. The sister is dead, too, and her property, so I understand, went to her son Tad Sobber."

"This is getting deep," said Tom, his sunny face growing wrinkled.

"It will soon get deeper, Tom. During the time that the firm of Stanhope, Robertson & Merrick were carrying freight from the West Indies there was a fierce revolution in Central America. Some families of high rank were forced to flee, among them a nobleman named Parmonelli, who left home carrying with him gold and diamonds worth many thousands of dollars. He managed to get on board one of the vessels owned by Mr. Stanhope's firm, and Mr. Stanhope was on the ship at the same time. The vessel was followed by revolutionists who were no better than pirates, and after a fierce fight the revolutionists shot Parmonelli and carried off his fortune."

"This is certainly getting deep," murmured Sam.

"Parmonelli was not killed at once, but died two days after being shot down. He was very bitter against the revolutionists, and said they had no right to take his fortune from him—that it was his and did not belong to the state. As Mr. Stanhope had befriended him to the last he made a will, leaving the fortune to Mr. Stanhope if the same could be recovered."

"And how much was it?" questioned Dick.

"I cannot say exactly the will mentions six bags of gold and one bag of precious stones, all packed in several chests."

"It's queer I never heard of this from Dora," said Dick. "She told me about the other money her father left."

"Mr. Stanhope kept the matter to himself, and at his death told only Mr. Laning, for—as you know—Mrs. Stanhope was then in delicate health and it was deemed very unwise to excite her."

"But what about the fortune—was it recovered?" asked Tom.

"No."

"Then the money has long since been spent," cried Sam in dismay.

"No, Sam, the money and the jewels, to the best of my belief, have never been touched. When the revolutionists carried them off they said they were going straight back to Central America with them. Instead, however, they landed on an island of the West Indies and there started to divide the fortune. This caused a bitter fight, in which several of the party were killed and wounded. Then it was decided to hide the money and jewels in a cave on the island and make a division later. A place was selected and the gold and jewels placed under heavy rocks in a small cave. After that the party sailed away. When they got home, much to their surprise and dismay, they found their country in the hands once more of the government. They were captured and all but two were sentenced to be shot as traitors. The two were sent to prison and they were released less than a year ago. One was a Spaniard named Doranez and the other a Spanish American sailor named Camel, but usually called Bahama Jack, because he has spent nearly all his life among the Bahama Islands."

"Did those two men go after the treasure when they got out of prison?" asked Sam.

"They wanted to, but were poor and had forgotten the exact location of the island where the treasure was hidden. Bahama Jack was a happy go lucky sort of a sailor and he came to this country and worked for a while on a lumber schooner running from Florida to Boston. Doranez also came to this country, but where he kept himself at first I do not know."

"Go on, Dad, this is getting exciting," broke in Tom, as his parent paused in his recital.

"Not long ago Mrs. Stanhope came to me for advice concerning this matter. Mr. Laning had told her everything, and she wanted to know if it would be worth while to organize an expedition to hunt for the treasure. I said I would look into the matter and ask her to give me what papers Mr. Stanhope had left in reference to the affair. I started to hunt up Bahama Jack and Doranez. After a good deal of work I found the former and had several long talks with him."

"Did you get any news from him?" asked Dick.

"A little. He does not remember exactly where the island was located, but told much about its general appearance and what other islands were in that vicinity. But he also told me something else, which worried me a good deal. It was that Sid Merrick, as the heir of Silas Merrick, was also after the treasure."

CHAPTER VII.
IN WHICH SOMETHING IS MISSING

"Sid Merrick after the treasure!" cried Dick.

"Yes. He wants it both for himself and for his nephew, Tad Sobber. He claims that the revolutionists took it from a ship belonging in part to his brother and consequently he has as much right to it as has Mrs. Stanhope."

"But that isn't so, is it?" asked Sam.

"No; the treasure, if it is found, belongs to Mr. Stanhope's estate absolutely—that is, to Mrs. Stanhope, Dora and the Lanings. The fact that Silas Merrick had an interest in the ship at the time of the stealing of the wealth cuts no figure at all."

"What is Sid Merrick doing?" asked Tom.

"He has been working in secret, looking for Bahama Jack and the Spaniard, Doranez. I found out that he had one talk with Bahama Jack, but the sailor did not like Merrick and told him very little. Then I started to find Doranez—he is the man I have been after during the past week. I found him and he promised to work with me if I would pay him for his trouble. But yesterday he sent me a note, stating he had changed his mind and was going to Spain, to look up some of his relatives. So he is probably out of it from now on."

"Maybe he is going to look for the treasure on his own account," suggested Randolph Rover.

"He cannot do that very well, for he has little or no money."

"And what do you propose to do, father—go on a hunt for the treasure?" asked Dick.

"Yes. From what papers I have on hand and the information gotten from Bahama Jack I think we stand a fair chance of locating that island and of finding the cave where the treasure is secreted. Of course, there is a good deal of guess work about it, but I am convinced the thing is worth trying."

"And how are you going at it?" came from Tom.

"A friend of mine in Philadelphia, a Mr. Dale, has a steam yacht which he is not going to use this summer, as he is going to Europe. I have determined to charter that yacht and go on a cruise among the West Indies. It will be a fine outing for the summer, even if we don't locate Treasure Isle, as Mr. Stanhope called the spot."

"And you'll take us along?" asked Tom, quickly.

"If you want to go."

"If we want to go? Does a duck want to swim, or a dog want to scratch fleas? Of course we want to go."

"Such a trip will suit me to a T," said Sam. "And I hope with all my heart we locate that treasure," he added earnestly.

"Of course you'll take this Bahama Jack along," said Dick.

"Yes, and I have promised him a big reward if the treasure is recovered," answered his father.

"Who else will be in the party?"

At this question Anderson Rover's eyes began to sparkle.

"I was going to keep it a secret, but perhaps I had better tell you. The steam yacht is a large one and can readily accommodate fifteen or twenty passengers. I have decided to ask Mrs. Stanhope to go and bring Dora, and will also ask the Lanings. Then they will know exactly what is being done to recover the treasure. In addition, if you want to take some of your chums with you, as you did on that houseboat trip."

"Hurrah, just the thing!" burst out Sam. "Let us take Fred Garrison by all means."

"Yes, and Songbird Powell and Hans Mueller" added Tom. "They will help to make things lively."

"Can they go?" questioned Dick.

"We can telegraph and find out," answered Tom. "I'll telegraph this afternoon," he added always ready to do things on the rush. "We ought to get an answer to night or to morrow morning.

"When do you want to start on the trip?" asked Dick.

"As soon as the party can be made up, and the steam yacht can be gotten in readiness. I have already instructed the captain to provision her for the trip."

"Then she has a captain and a crew?"

"Oh, Yes, she carries ten men, including an engineer and his assistant."

"That is certainly fine!" said Dick, and he smiled as he thought of what a nice trip they would have with Dora Stanhope on board. Dick was not "moonstruck," but he had a manly regard for Dora that did him credit.

After that Anderson Rover gave them many more details regarding the treasure, and his talks with Bahama Jack and of what he hoped to accomplish. He had a fair idea of the latitude and longitude of Treasure Isle, which, he had been told, was of coral formation, covered with palms and shaped somewhat like a horseshoe.

"Bahama Jack says the treasure cave is about in the center of the inner curve of the island, but that you cannot sail close to it on account of the numerous reefs. You have to land on the island in a small boat, and that is why very few ships stop there. Natives of that vicinity occasionally go there for fruit and for birds, but there is no regular village on the island."

"If the island is shaped like a horseshoe we ought not to have great difficulty in locating it," said Dick.

"The trouble is, you cannot see the formation very well from the sea, Dick. If one were in a balloon it would be different. You must remember that there are many hundreds of islands scattered in that part of our globe."

"Let's take a balloon along," suggested Tom. "Then we could go up and take a look around."

"You couldn't look far enough, Tom, and if you tried to sail in the balloon you'd probably drop into the ocean and be drowned. No, we'll have to do our searching from the steam yacht. But I have several maps and drawings which I think, will aid us."

"The things Cuffer and Shelley were after?" cried Dick.

"Perhaps if they are in league with Sid Merrick. Merrick, of course, would like to get all the information possible."

"I'd like to look at the maps and drawings."

"So would I," added Sam and Tom. The idea of going on a treasure hunt filled them with great interest.

"The maps and drawings I have are only copies," went on Anderson Rover. "The originals are in Mrs. Stanhope's possession."

Mr. Rover turned to his brother. "You have them, Randolf. Will you please get them?"

"I have them?" queried Randolph Rover, in perplexity. As my old readers know, he was at times somewhat absent minded.

"Why, yes, don't you remember my giving them to you? They were in a large yellow envelope. I think you placed them away with your traction company bonds."

"Why—er—so I did," stammered Randolph Rover. "But I—er—I don't quite remember what I did with them." He scratched his head. "I'll go and get my tin box."

He left the sitting room, and after being gone fully ten minutes returned with a flat tin box, in which he kept some papers of value.

"The envelope doesn't seem to be here," he said, turning over the contents of the box.

"Don't you remember it?" asked his brother, anxiously.

"Oh, yes, I remember it very well now. I saw it only a couple of days before I went to Carwell with my bonds."

"Did you take that tin box to Carwell?" asked Tom.

"Yes."

"Was the envelope in it then?"

"I—er—I really don't know, Thomas. You see I was much upset, thinking my bonds were no good. Perhaps the yellow envelope was in the box, under the bonds."

"And did Sid Merrick have hold of the box?" demanded Anderson Rover.

"He may have had. The box was on a side table, and he walked around the room and over to it several times."

"Then, unless you have the envelope now, Sid Merrick stole it," said Anderson Rover, somewhat bitterly.

This announcement filled Randolph Rover with increased anxiety and as a result he looked over all his private papers and ransacked his safe and his desk from end to end. But the precious yellow envelope and its contents were not brought to light.

"Merrick must have gotten hold of that envelope at the time he stole the bonds," said Dick. "Maybe that is what made him trace up this story of the treasure."

"That may be true, Dick," answered his parent.

Randolph Rover was greatly distressed over the disappearance of the maps and drawings and upbraided himself roundly for not having been more careful.

"Now that they are in this Merrick's hands he may make use of them," he said dolefully.

"Undoubtedly he will," answered Anderson Rover.

"If he has those papers and maps why did he send Cuffer and Shelley here?" asked Tom.

"Most likely he thought he could get additional information."

"It seems to me the best thing we can do is to get after that treasure without delay," said Dick. "If we don't, Merrick may form some kind of a party, locate the island, and steal the gold and jewels from under our very noses!"

"Oh, such things are not done in a day, Dick," said his father, with a faint smile. "But I agree with you, the quicker we get after the treasure the better."

After that a discussion lasting well after the dinner hour followed, and was only ended when Mrs. Rover fairly drove them into the dining room for the midday repast. It was resolved that the party to go in search of the treasure should be made up of Anderson Rover and his three sons, Mrs. Stanhope and Dora, the Lannings, and also Fred Garrison, Songbird Powell and Hans Mueller. During the afternoon a number of telegrams and letters were written, and the boys send these off before nightfall.

Aleck Pop was very much interested in such conversation as he had overheard, and as he had accompanied the boys to the jungles of Africa and on the houseboat trip he was very anxious to be a member of the present party.

"I don't see how yo' young gen'men is gwine to get along widout me," he said to Sam. "Don't yo' think you kin squeeze me aboadh somehow?"

"Aren't you afraid you'd get seasick, Aleck?" asked Sam.

"I ain't afraid ob muffin, if only yo'll take me along," answered the darkey earnestly.

"I suppose the steam yacht has its cook."

"Dat might be, Massa Sam, but didn't I cook all right on dot houseboat?"

"You certainly did."

"Might be as how I could gab dot cook on de yacht seem p'ints as to wot yo' young gen'men like, ain't dot so?"

"Perhaps, Aleck. If you wish, I'll speak to father about it."

"T'ank yo' werry much, Massa Sam!"

"But you must promise one thing," put Tom, who was listening to the talk.

"Wot is dat?"

"You won't run off and marry the widow Taylor when you get back."

"Huh! I'se done wid dat trash!" snorted Aleck. "She kin mahrry dat Thomas an' welcome. I don't want her or her chillun neither!"

"All right, then, Aleck, we'll, see what we can do for you," said Tom, and Sam said the same. In the end it was agreed that Aleck should accompany the party as a general helper, and this pleased the colored man very much. It was a lucky thing for the boys that Aleck went along, as certain later events proved.

CHAPTER VIII.
THE ROVER BOYS IN NEW YORK

The more the Rover boys talked about the treasure hunt the more enthusiastic they became, until, as Tom expressed it, they were "simply boiling over with enthusiasm."

"It will be a grand thing for the Stanhopes and the Lanings if we do locate that treasure," said Sam. "Mr. Laning has some money, but I know he'd like more, so he wouldn't have to farm quite so hard."

"And Dick wants to get all he can for Dora, I'm certain of that," said Tom, with a merry glance at his elder brother.

"How about you getting the Laning share for Nellie's benefit?" retorted Dick, his face growing red. "I reckon the boot is as long as the shoe."

As the Rovers had plenty of money it was an easy matter to arrange for the expenses of the trip. Mrs. Stanhope wanted to pay a share, but Anderson Rover said she had better wait until the treasure was found.

Inside of three, days word was received from all those who had been asked to participate in the search. Mr. Laning said that he could not leave his farm very well, but that his wife and two daughters would go. Mrs. Stanhope and Dora said they would pack immediately. Fred Garrison was visiting Hans Mueller and the two sent a telegram as follows:

"You couldn't hold us back if you tried. Where shall we meet you?"

"That's like Fred," said Dick. "I am awfully glad he is to be with us —and glad Hans will come, too."

The last telegram to come in was from Songbird Powell. The reply of the would-be poet of Putnam Hall was characteristic:

"Tell me where,
And I'll be there,
On the run
For lots of fun."

"If that isn't Songbird!" exclaimed Sam, laughing, as he read the telegram. "Had to talk in rhyme even over the telegraph wire!"

It was finally decided that the whole party should meet in Philadelphia about the Fourth of July, which was now less than a week off. They should go directly to the steam yacht, and the voyage was to begin as soon as all arrangements were completed.

"I wish to stop off at New York for a day," said Anderson Rover. "If you boys want to go with me you may do so."

"That will suit me," answered Dick, and his brothers said the same.

It had been agreed that no outsiders should be told of the treasure hunt, so nothing was mentioned but a summer trip on a steam yacht. The day the Rovers and Aleck Pop left the farm was a clear one, and all were in the best of spirits. The colored man drove to the depot with Jack Ness and the trunks and dress suit cases, and all of the others went in the carryall, Randolph Rover driving and Mrs. Rover giving the boys final instructions about taking care of themselves.

"I shall miss you very much," she said, with tears in her eyes. Her lively nephews were as dear to her as if they were her own sons.

"You'd better go along, Aunt Martha," said Dick.

"We'd like it first rate," added Sam.

"It might help us to keep out of mischief," came from Tom, with a bright smile.

"No, I'll stay at home with your uncle, boys. But do take care of yourselves, and come home safe."

"Oh, there will be no danger in this trip," said Dick, but he was mistaken—there was to be great peril and of an unusual kind. If the treasure hunters could have seen what was before them they would not have started off in such a confident frame of mind.

The train was a little late, but presently it rolled into the station and the trunks and other baggage were hoisted aboard. Then came the final embraces and the boys climbed up the steps, followed by their father and Aleck.

"Hurrah, we are off at last!" cried Tom, and waved his cap enthusiastically. The others did the same, and then the train started and Oak Run quickly faded from sight. As the boys settled down in their seats a lad came from another car and moved swiftly toward them.

"Songbird, by all that's lucky!" cried Dick, and caught the other by the hand.

"I thought you'd be on this train," answered Songbird Powell. "I got your wire last night that you would stop off at New York. I am going to stop, too—to see an uncle of mine on a little business."

"Then you'll travel with us to Philadelphia?" queried Sam.

"Sure."

"Good! Tom was just saying he'd like some of the others along."

"When I got your invitation I danced a jig of delight," went on Songbird. "I just couldn't help it. Then I sat down and wrote—"

"A piece of poetry about it thirty five stanzas long," finished Tom.

"No, Tom, there are only six verses. You see I couldn't help it—I was so chuck full of enthusiasm. The poem begins like this:

"'Twas a peaceful, summer night,
When all the stars were shining bright,
There came a rap on our house door
Which made me leap from bed to floor.
To me had come a telegram
From my old chums, Dick, Tom and Sam
Asking if I had a notion
To sail with them upon the ocean.
To skim along on waters blue—"

"And then and there get seasick, too," finished Tom. "Don't forget to put in about the seasickness, Songbird—it always goes with a voyage, you know."

"Seasick!" snorted the would-be poet. "Who ever heard of seasickness in a poem? The next line is this:

"And see so many sights quite new,
To rest in quiet day by day
And watch the fishes at their play."

"That's the first verse. The second begins—"

"Save it, Songbird, until we're on the yacht," interrupted Sam. "We'll have more time to listen then."

"All right," answered the would-be poet cheerfully. "I want to fix up some of the lines anyhow. I've got 'harm' to rhyme with 'storm' and it doesn't quite suit me."

"Never mind—a storm often does great harm," said Dick. "You can easily fix it up by throwing out both words, you know."

After that the talk drifted around to the matter of the treasure hunt and Songbird was given some of the details, in which he became much interested. He declared that he thought the trip on the steam yacht would be even more interesting than the one on the houseboat had been.

"We're after something definite this trip," he said. "We've got something to look forward to specially if that Sid Merrick starts a rival hunt."

"We want to get ahead of Merrick," answered Dick. "We want to locate Treasure Isle and get the gold and jewels before he knows what we are up to."

"What's the name of the steam yacht."

"The *Rainbow*."

"That's a good name, for a rainbow is a sign of good promise," was Songbird's comment.

The party had to make one change of cars and had their dinner on the train. They arrived at the Grand Central Depot at half past two o'clock and the Rovers went to a nearby hotel, taking Aleck with them, while Songbird hurried off to transact his business with his uncle.

Mr. Rover had to meet some men who were interested in his mining ventures in the far west, and so, after accommodations had been obtained, he hurried off, leaving the boys to their own devices.

"Let us take a stroll down Broadway," suggested Sam, to whom the sights of this busy thoroughfare were always interesting.

The others were willing, and they passed through Forty second street to Broadway and then turned southward. The street was filled with wagons, trucks and trolley cars, and the sidewalk appeared to "overflow with folks," as Sam said. At one point a man was giving some sort of an exhibition in a store window and here the crowd was so great they had to walk out into the gutter to get past.

"I can tell you one thing," remarked Dick. "There is after all but one New York and no other city is like it."

The boys walked slowly as far as Union Square and then sat down on one of the park benches to rest. Nearly all the benches were filled with people and in idle curiosity Dick began to scan the various types of men present, from bright, brisk clerks to fat and unshaved bummers, too lazy to work.

"Hullo!"

Dick uttered the exclamation so abruptly that Sam and Tom were startled.

"What do you see?" queried both.

"Look there!"

They gazed in the direction Dick pointed out and on a distant bench saw a youth of about Tom's age, but heavier set, talking to a man who wore a rusty suit of brown and a peculiarly shaped slouch hat.

"Why, that's Tad Sobber!" cried Tom.

"So it is," added Sam. "Who is that fellow with him?"

"I don't know, although his figure looks somewhat familiar to me," answered Dick.

"What can Tad be doing in New York?" questioned Tom. "Do you suppose he is down here with Sid Merrick?"

"Perhaps."

"Let's go over and see what he has to say for himself," suggested Sam. "Maybe he'll run away when he sees us."

All of the boys were curious to know what the former bully of Putnam Hall might have to say for himself and they strode over to the bench upon which Sobber and the man in brown were sitting. They came up behind the pair.

"I can't give you any money, Cuffer," they heard Tad Sobber say. "You'll have to wait till my Uncle Sid gets here."

"When will he get to New York?"

"To morrow."

"That fellow is Cuffer, the man who ran away from us at the old mill!" cried Dick.

"Let us catch him and hand him over to the police," returned Tom.

In his excitement he talked rather loudly and this attracted the attention of Cuffer and Tad Sobber.

"The Rovers!" cried Sobber, leaping to his feet in consternation. "How did they get down to New York?"

"Who did you say?" questioned Cuffer, and then looking at the three youths his face blanched. "We must get away from here, and be quick about it!"

He started to run and Dick and Sam went after him. The chase led to the lower end of the little park, and then Cuffer crossed Fourteenth street, and amid the crowd bound homeward for the day, pushed his way in the direction of the Third Avenue elevated railroad station.

In the meantime Tad Sobber started to run in another direction. But before he had taken a dozen steps Tom was on him and had him by the arm.

"Stop, Sobber," he said shortly.

"I won't! You let me go, Tom Rover."

"I'll not let you go," answered Tom, firmly. "And if you don't stand still I'll call a policeman and have you arrested."

CHAPTER IX.
A CHASE ON THE BOWERY

Tom's threat to have Tad Sobber arrested caused the former bully of the school to pause and turn pale.

"You—er—you don't mean that," he faltered. "You can't have me arrested."

"We'll see about that, Sobber."

"I haven't done anything wrong."

"Then why did you run away from Putnam Hall?"

"I had a right to leave. Captain Putnam wasn't treating me fairly."

"You ran away on account of that snake affair—you can't deny it."

"Humph!"

"That snake nearly killed Nick Pell. He isn't over it yet, altogether."

"Bah! It wasn't the snake made Nick sick. He wasn't feeling well some days before the snake bit him."

"It was the snake and nothing else put him in bed," answered Tom warmly. "And that is not all. You are in league with your uncle, who robbed my uncle of those traction company bonds."

"I—er—I don't know anything about that matter," answered Sobber, hastily.

"Well, I know all about it. You were with your uncle when he got away from us, and when he dropped the pocketbook containing the bonds."

"Did you get the bonds back?" asked Sobber, with sudden interest. It may be added here that Sid Merrick had gone back long after the chase to look for the pocketbook, but, of course, had been unable to get any trace of it.

"We did."

"My uncle didn't steal them. Your uncle put them in his hands to sell," went on Tad Sobber, with sudden boldness. "It is all a cooked up story about his running away with them. And it's a cooked up story about his having anything to do with those freight thieves. My uncle is an honest man."

"I know all about the freight affair, for I overheard him talking to some of the other thieves," answered Tom. "Where is your uncle now?"

"Do you think I'd be fool enough to tell you?"

"Perhaps you might—if I had you locked up."

"My uncle is a good long way from New York."

"I heard you tell that man your uncle would be in the city tomorrow."

"I didn't say any such thing!" burst out Sobber, but his manner showed that he was very much disturbed.

"You did say it. Where are you stopping?"

"Nowhere—I only got in a few hours ago."

"Did you come here to meet Cuffer?"

"What do you know about Cuffer?"

"I know your uncle hired him and a man named Shelley to visit our farm and get some things belonging to my father."

"Why, you're crazy! My uncle hardly knows Cuffer—and I never heard of a man named Shelley."

"I am not crazy, and you know I am speaking the truth," answered Tom, calmly. "Now you tell me where your uncle is or I'll have you arrested."

"You'll not arrest me!" exclaimed Tad Sobber, and with a sudden movement he twisted himself free from Tom's grasp. "You follow me and you'll get the worst of it!" he added, and darted across the park at top speed.

Tom made after the bully, but as luck would have it a nurse girl with a baby carriage got between them and before Tom could clear himself of the carriage Sobber was a good distance away. He turned to the eastward, down a side street where a large building was in the course of erection. He looked back and then skipped into the unfinished building.

"He shan't catch me," he muttered to himself, and ran to the rear of the building, amid piles of bricks and concrete blocks. A number of workmen were present, but nobody noticed him.

Reaching the building Tom peered inside, but saw nothing of the bully. He was about to go in when a warning cry reached him from overhead.

"Get back there, unless you want to be hurt!"

Tom looked up and saw a workman in the act of throwing down a mass of rubbish, broken bricks, sticks and old mortar. He leaped back and the stuff descended in front of him and raised a cloud of dust.

"What do you want here, young man?" demanded the superintendent of the building as he came forward.

"I am after a boy who just ran in here."

"Nobody here that I saw."

"He just came in."

"We don't allow skylarking around here. You make yourself scarce," and the superintendent waved Tom away.

"I want to have that fellow arrested—that is why he ran away from me."

"Oh, that's a different thing. Go find him, if you can."

The superintendent stepped aside and Tom entered the building. But the delay had cost him dear, for in the meanwhile Tad Sobber had made good his escape by running back to the next street. Tom looked around for over quarter of an hour and then gave up the chase.

"It's too bad, but it can't be helped," he mused. "I may as well go back to the park and wait for Dick and Sam. I hope they caught that Cuffer."

While Tom was talking to Sobber the other Rover boys had followed Cuffer to the elevated railroad station. A train was just coming in and Cuffer bounded up the steps two at a time, with the boys not far behind.

"Stop that man!" cried Dick, to the crowd coming from the train. But before anybody would or could act, Cuffer had slipped past the man at the ticket box and was trying to board one of the cars. Dick essayed to follow, but the ticket box guard stopped him.

"Not to fast, young fellow. Where's your ticket?"

"I must catch that man—he is wanted by the police," answered Dick.

"That's an old dodge, but it don't work with me, see? You go back and get a ticket," said the gateman, firmly.

"But he'll get away from me," pleaded the eldest Rover.

"If he does, it's not my fault. You can't pass here without a ticket."

By this time the train was almost ready to start. But Sam had procured tickets and he rushed up.

"There are two tickets!" he cried. "Come on, Dick!" and he sprinted for the train.

The guard was closing the platform gate, but they managed to squeeze through. The train was crowded with people going home from their day's work and in the jam they could see nothing of Cuffer.

"But he is on board," said Dick.

"I know it," returned his brother, "and we must find him. Quick, you go to the front and I'll go to the rear. If you locate him, tell the trainman you want him arrested at the next station."

Without another word the brothers separated and each tried to work his way to an end of the train, which was composed of five cars. This was by no means easy, for the crowd was in no humor to be jostled or have its toes stepped upon.

"Look where you are going!" cried one stout man to Sam. "Stop pushing me!" And then as the youngest Rover dodged out of his way he ran his ear into the big feather on a young lady clerk's immense hat. The girl glared at him and murmured something under her breath, which was far from complimentary. By the time he had reached the front end of the car half a dozen passengers were his enemies.

Dick had gone to the rear and as he entered the last car he saw Cuffer crouching down in a seat near the door. The train was stopping at another station, and quick as a flash the fellow arose in the seat, shot between Dick and a man with several bundles, and forced his way out on the platform. Dick tried to follow, but was caught fast by several men.

"Here, don't be acting in such a rowdy fashion!" cried one man, in great irritation.

"You knocked my bundle from my hand!" added another. "It's a shame the way some roughs act on these trains. The authorities ought to have them arrested," he went on in a loud voice.

"What's the trouble in there?" demanded a policeman, who was on the station platform in the crowd.

"This young fellow is too fresh," explained the man who had dropped his bundle.

"I want to get off, that's all," said Dick.

"Well, you behave yourself," growled the guardian of the peace, and Dick was glad enough to get away with this reprimand. He saw Cuffer running for the stairs and made after him as rapidly as the density of the crowd permitted.

When Dick gained the street once more the train bearing Sam was again on its way downtown. Cuffer was about a block away, running past Cooper Institute in the direction of the Bowery.

"I may as well keep up the chase and try to run him down," thought Dick, but he wished his brother was with him.

At this time of day the Bowery, always a busy thoroughfare, was swarming with people, and the numerous "barkers" for the clothing stores, photograph establishments, and the like, were doing their best to make trade come to them. As Dick hurried past one clothing establishment a short, stocky Jew stepped in front of him.

"Von't you step inside, young chentleman? I sell you some gloding cheap as dirt."

"I don't want any clothing," answered Dick, briefly.

"I vos mof next veek, und I sell you a suit for next to nodding," persisted the clothing dealer.

"I don't want to buy anything," said Dick, and tried to push past the man. The fellow caught him by the arm.

"If you vill only look at dose peautiful suits vot I haf for twelf dollar—"

The Jew got no further, for with a strong push Dick sent him staggering among the dummies in front of his store. He tried to recover his balance, but could not, and over he went, bringing down two of the dummies on top of him.

"Serves you right," flung back Dick, as he ran on. "The next time you'll know enough to leave me alone."

"Isaac! Moses! Sthop dot young mans!" bawled the clothing dealer, as he scrambled to his feet. "He has ruined two peautiful dummies, mit fine suits on! Sthop him!"

"Not to day!" muttered Dick, and dodged into the crowd. Then, seeing that Cuffer had crossed the street, he did the same, and continued the pursuit on that side.

But to follow anybody long in a crowd on the Bowery is not easy, and after six blocks had been passed Dick came to a halt on a corner in bewilderment. He had seen Cuffer last on that corner, but where the rascal had gone was a question.

"Want a paper?" asked an urchin close by. "Evening papers!"

"Say, kid, did you see a man run past here just now?" asked Dick.

"Sure I did."

"Where did he go?"

"Wot will yer give me if I tell yer?" asked the newsboy shrewdly.

"Five cents."

"All right, hand over de nickel."

"Here it is," and Dick showed the money in his hand. "Now where was it?"

"He went in de Sunrise Hotel, down dare. I watched him run in."

"What kind of a hat did he have on?"

"A soft hat wid a big knock in one side."

"And you are sure he went in that hotel?"

"Cross me heart, mister. I watched him, cos he was out o' breath, an' I knowed he was up to som't'in'."

"Here is your money," answered Dick, and passed the nickel over. Then he walked to the hotel and paused on the sidewalk to look the place over before entering.

CHAPTER X.
DICK BECOMES A PRISONER

The Sunrise Hotel had seen better days. It was a five story brick building, blackened by age and had numerous small windows, down in front of which ran an iron fire escape. The lower floor was used as a drinking place, to one side of which ran a narrow stairs, leading to an office and a parlor above.

Looking in over the short doors of the drinking place, Dick saw that Cuffer was not there. He rightly surmised that the fellow had gone upstairs, to a room he was occupying.

"Perhaps that fellow Shelley is with him," mused Dick. "If so, I'd like to collar them both."

Several men were coming and going and nobody paid particular attention to the youth until he gained the dingy office, where two men were smoking and talking over the merits of some race horses.

"What can I do for you?" asked one of the men abruptly, as Dick looked around.

"Is a man named Cuffer stopping here?"

The hotel clerk shook his head.

"Perhaps I have the name wrong. I mean a man who came in a minute or two ago—fellow with a soft hat, knocked in on the side."

"Oh, that chap! Yes, he's here—room eighteen, next floor," and the clerk pointed up the stairs, for the hotel had no elevator.

Dick walked up the stairs slowly, revolving in his mind what he should do if he met Cuffer face to face. If he had the man arrested it might lead to legal complications, and the voyage in search of Treasure Isle might be delayed. It would be hard to prove that the rascal had done any actual wrong.

Reaching the upper hallway, Dick looked at the dingy numbers on the still more dingy doors. Eighteen proved to be at the rear, where it was so dark he could scarcely see.

As the youth approached the door he heard a murmur of voices in the room beyond. He listened, and made out Cuffer speaking, and then he recognized the voice of Shelley.

"And so I dusted out before I had a chance to get any money from Sobber," Cuffer was saying.

"Well, did the Rovers catch the young fellow?" questioned Shelley.

"That I don't know. If he didn't know enough to run away he is a fool."

"You say one of the Rovers followed you from the train?"

"Yes, but I gave him the slip as soon as I reached the Bowery," answered Cuffer with a chuckle.

"Well, what are we to do next?" asked Shelley, after a pause.

"There is nothing to do but to wait until tomorrow, when Merrick arrives."

"Have you any faith in this treasure hunt of his?"

"I have so long as he pays the bills. I wouldn't put a cent of my own money in it."

"Has he got enough money to see the thing through?"

"So he says. He met the captain of that tramp vessel somewhere and got him interested in the hunt by promising him a share of the find. He says as soon as he can get hold of a Spaniard who knows the exact location of the island he'll set sail."

"And take the Spaniard along?"

"Of course. The Spaniard was one of the chaps who originally took the treasure to the island."

"Well, where do we come in?"

"He wants us along because he is afraid the fellows on the vessel will make a fight for the gold and jewels when they are found. Some of those sailors are pretty bloodthirsty, you know. He says he is going to take at least four strong men whom he can trust."

Dick listened with keen interest to this talk, which revealed a great deal. Sid Merrick had made an arrangement to go on a voyage after the treasure! How soon he would start there was no telling, but probably as quickly as he could get ready. More than this, he expected to have with him the Spaniard, Doranez, the fellow who had said he was going to Spain to visit his relatives. More than likely Merrick and Doranez were in league with each other and would do all in their power to keep the treasure out of the hands of the rightful owners.

"If only Tom and Sam were here," thought Dick. "Or if only Tom has captured Tad Sobber. This is getting lively, to say the least."

The men were now speaking in a lower tone and he put his ear to the keyhole, to catch what they might say. Then, of a sudden, the door opened and he found himself confronted by Shelley.

"Thought I heard somebody in the hall!" cried that individual, and grabbed Dick by the arm.

"Let go!" answered the youth and tried to break away. But Cuffer came to Shelley's assistance, and between them the two men dragged the boy into the room and shut the door after him. Dick struggled vigorously even when in the apartment until Cuffer caught up an empty water pitcher and flourished it over his head.

"Make another move and I'll knock you senseless with this!" he exclaimed and the look on his face showed he meant what he said. Seeing his captors were too powerful for him, Dick subsided and was forced into a chair in a corner.

"Been listening to all our talk, I suppose," said Cuffer, uglily. He was angry to think that Dick had been able to follow him after all.

"I have," was the youth's bold reply. He felt nothing was to be gained by beating around the bush.

"It's a nice business to be in!"

"It is better than the business you are in."

"I don't think so."

"I do. You fellows are in league with Sid Merrick, and you know what sort he is."

"See here," interrupted Shelley. "Now we have him in here, what are we going to do with him?"

"You are going to let me out," said Dick.

"Perhaps we are," said Cuffer, and gave Shelley a significant look.

"Let us see if he's got any papers with him," suggested Shelley, and returned the look given to him by his companion.

The look meant that they would go through Dick's pockets and rob him. The men were thorough rascals and if the youth had anything worth taking they meant to have it.

"You keep out of my pockets!" cried Dick and started to rise from the chair in which he was sitting. Instantly both men grabbed him, and while Cuffer held him tightly from the rear, Shelley caught up a towel and gagged him. Then a bed sheet was used to tie Dick inside of a closet in a corner of the room.

"Listen, I think somebody is coming!" cried Cuffer, in sudden alarm.

"Keep the boy quiet!" answered Shelley and ran to the hall door just as a knock sounded upon it.

"What's the racket up here?" demanded the voice of the hotel clerk.

"Oh, we were only trying a vaudeville turn," answered Shelley, coolly. "We have an engagement for next week."

"Well, stop that noise and don't break any of the furniture, or you'll pay for it," growled the clerk and went away. It chanced that actors occasionally stopped at the hotel and practised their parts. Shelley knew of this, hence the excuse he gave for the noise made in rendering Dick a prisoner.

As soon as the clerk had retired Cuffer and Shelley both paid their attention to Dick, and with great rapidity they went through his pockets, stripping him of his watch and chain, and twenty four dollars and a quarter in money. They also took a small diamond scarf pin and a ring set with a valuable ruby. In one pocket Cuffer found several letters and he likewise appropriated these.

"Not such a bad haul," was the thief's comment.

Of course, Dick did not submit willingly, but with a gag in his mouth, and his hands and feet tied tightly, he could do but little. As soon as the men had taken his things from him, they shut the closet door upon him and locked it. A few minutes later all became quiet, showing that they had left the room.

The closet was small and stuffy and in this warm weather made Dick perspire freely. But without waiting to make certain that the men were really gone, he commenced to work upon his bonds and the gag in his mouth.

It was no light task and it was a good quarter of an hour before he got one hand loose.

Then he freed his other hand and undid the troublesome gag, which had all but smothered him, and then unfastened his feet.

He was still a prisoner in the closet, the door of which was an old fashioned one and thick. But by bracing his feet against the back wall, Dick got a firm hold and soon his shoulder on the barrier caused it to bend and creak. Then the lock gave way and the door flew open with a bang.

A glance around the room showed that the men had flown, and for good, for two valises which had stood in a corner were missing.

Dick leaped to the hall door, only to find it locked from the outside.

"They must have gone that way," he reasoned, after a look out of the window, and then he rapped on the door loudly.

It was several minutes before anybody answered his summons. Then an ignorant looking chambermaid appeared.

"Phot does yez want?" she demanded, in a strong Irish brogue.

"I am locked in. Let me out," answered Dick.

After some fumbling, the chambermaid found her key and unlocked the door. She gazed at Dick in some surprise, for she saw that he was excited.

"Sure, I didn't know yez had that room," she said.

"Did you see the two men who had this room?" demanded the youth.

"I did not."

"They robbed me and ran away."

"Saints preserve us! Robbed ye? Of phat?"

"Of everything I had. Sure you didn't see 'em?"

"Not since this marnin'."

"Well, they must have just gone out," said Dick, and ran down the stairs and to the office. Here he found the place deserted, the clerk having gone down to the dining room for his supper, and nobody else being on duty. The clerk listened to his story with small interest and shrugged his shoulders.

"Don't see what I can do," he said. "We ain't responsible for our guests. You had better go and see the police. I hope you catch them, for such rascals give hotels bad reputations."

"Do you know the men at all?"

"No, never set eyes on 'em until a couple of days ago. Then they came in, hired that room, and came and went to suit themselves. One was named Brown and the other Smith—at least that's the names on the register."

"Those were fake names. Then you won't help me to catch them?"

"I don't see what I can do," answered the clerk, calmly. "We are not to blame for this, you can see that for yourself."

Dick could see, and after a few words more, he left the hotel, feeling very depressed in spirits. He spent an hour in looking up and down the Bowery for Cuffer and Shelley, but without success. Then, as it was getting late, he returned to the hotel at which he and the rest of his family were putting up.

CHAPTER XI.
ABOARD THE STEAM YACHT

Mr Rover, as well as Tom and Sam, had come in, and all were anxious to hear what Dick might have to report. They were filled with amazement at the story of the robbery.

"I thought I'd wait about telling the police until I had heard what you had to say," said Dick, to his father.

"I am afraid in a big city like New York it won't do much good to tell the police," answered Anderson Rover. "However, we can report it to morrow. But I think Cuffer and Shelley will keep in the shade until they see Sid Merrick and have a chance to get away," and in this surmise Mr. Rover was correct. The matter was reported to the police, and that was the end of it, so far as the authorities went, for they failed to apprehend the evildoers.

Mr. Rover was much worried when he learned that Merrick had fallen in with a captain of a tramp vessel who was ready to go on a hunt for the treasure. And he was still more worried when Dick told him of the letters which had been abstracted from his coat pocket by the thieves. Among them was one from Mrs. Stanhope mentioning the treasure hunt and how she would be on hand at Philadelphia to board the steam yacht with Dora and the Lanings.

"If Cuffer and Shelley turn that letter over to Merrick it will give him some idea of our proposed trip," said Mr. Rover, "and more than likely he will strain every nerve to get ahead of us."

"His vessel may not be able to sail as fast as our steam yacht," said Tom.

"That is true, Tom, but he may get down among the West Indies before we can locate Treasure Isle and then he'll have as good a chance as ourselves. Moreover, if he should land on the isle at the time we did —"

"There'd be a hot time, that's sure," said the fun-loving boy, with a grin.

"Do you think they'd fight?" asked Sam.

"Yes, if they saw a chance of getting the best Of us," answered his father.

"I wish I had caught Tad Sobber," came from Tom, regretfully.

"That might have done some good, but I doubt it," said Anderson Rover. "From what I have learned of this Sid Merrick he is a man bound to do as he sees fit, regardless of those around him. When the freight thieves were captured he managed to get away, and he'll try to get away even if we catch Tad, Cuffer, and Shelley."

"I guess he is a worse man than Arnold Baxter was," was Dick's comment. He referred to an old enemy of the Rovers, who had now reformed.

"Much worse than either Mr. Baxter or his son Dan ever were," answered Mr. Rover. "If caught in a corner I think this Merrick would be capable of any wicked thing."

"What do you advise?" asked Tom.

"We will go to Philadelphia as soon as possible and get the steam yacht ready for the trip. The best way to foil Merrick and his crowd is to find the isle, get possession of the treasure, and get away before they know what we are doing," answered Anderson Rover.

On the following day the party was rejoined by Songbird, and then all journeyed to Philadelphia, taking Aleck Pop with them. They found the *Rainbow* tied up to a dock along the Delaware River, and went aboard. The master of the craft, Captain Barforth, was on hand to greet them, and he speedily made them feel at home. The captain was a big, good natured man of about forty, and the boys knew they would like him the moment they saw him.

"Well, this is certainly a swell boat," said Sam, after an inspection. "And as clean as a whistle."

"Puts me in mind of the deserted steam yacht we boarded in the Gulf of Mexico," answered Dick, referring to a happening which has been related in detail in "The Rover Boys in Southern Waters."

"Wonder if we'll have as many adventures as we did on that boat," mused Dick. "Those were hot times, eh?"

"We'll not lack for adventures if we come into contact with Merrick and his gang," answered Songbird, who had been told all the details of the adventures in New York.

There were six single and four double staterooms aboard the steam yacht, so the Rovers and their friends were not crowded for accommodations, since even a single room contained two berths, an upper and a lower. Each room was done in white and gold, giving, it a truly aristocratic appearance. There was a good deal of brass and nickel plated work, and the metal shone like a mirror.

"I declare it's most too good to use," said Sam, when on a tour of inspection. "This craft must have cost a sight of money."

"It did," answered his father. "But the owner is a millionaire so he can well afford it."

The boys were as much interested in the machinery as in anything, and they visited the engine room and became acquainted with Frank Norton, the head engineer. They learned that the engine was of the most modern type, and that the *Rainbow*, in spite of her breadth of beam she was rather wide could make twenty to twenty six knots an hour in an ordinary sea.

"And we've got a licence to go where we please," added the head engineer proudly.

Now that they were aboard the steam yacht the Rover boys were anxious to be sailing. But they were also anxious to greet their friends and they awaited the arrival of the others with interest. Fred Garrison and Hans Mueller came in together, the following noon, Hans lugging a dress suit case that was as big almost as a dog house.

"Here we are again!" sang out Fred, dropping his baggage and shaking hands all around. "I declare it's like when we went on the houseboat trip."

"Maybe I ton't vos glad to drop dot leetle drunk alretty?" said Hans, indicating his baggage. "He vos veigh most a don, I dink."

"Why didn't you let an expressman bring it?" asked Dick.

"Not much!" declared the German youth, shaking his head vigorously. "Vonce I haf a pox mid a new hat in him, und I say to a poy, carry dot und I gif you den cents. Vell he is carrying dot yet, I dink, for I ton't see dot hat no more, nefer!"

"Well, you won't have to carry any more baggage for a long while to come," said Mr. Rover, with a smile, and then had Aleck take the things below. When Hans saw the elegant staterooms, and the main saloon of the steam yacht with its beautiful mirrors and rich carvings, his eyes bulged out like saucers.

"Mine cracious!" he gasped. "Vos dis der poat we sail in, udder vos dis a poat pelonging to Mr. Vanderfellow, or some of dose udder millionaires?"

"This is the boat," said Tom, with a wink at the others. "Of course it's rather plain, Hans, but maybe you'll get used to it."

"Blain? Vy, Dom—"

"There are only six kinds of baths aboard, cold, hot, soda, milk, mustard, and cream de fizz, but if you want any other kind all you've got to do is to ask the ship's carpenter about it."

"Six kinds of paths! Vy I ton't vos—"

"And then at meals the cook serves only five kinds of dessert pie, fruit, iced cabbage, vinegar sherbit, and hot lardalumpabus. Of course I know you don't like pie and fruit and things like that, but you'll fall dead in love with the lardalumpabus," went on the fun-loving Rover.

"Vot is dot lardapusalump ennahow?" queried Hans, scratching his head gravely. "I ton't remember him."

"Why, it's a compote, with frizzled gizzardinus and pollylolly. It's delicious, served with cream and salt—but you want lots of salt, Hans, lots of salt."

"Maybe I try him, I ton't know," answered the German youth, gravely. And then even Tom had to turn away, to keep from roaring in Hans' face.

The Rover boys went to the depot to meet the train which was to bring in the Stanhopes and the Lanings. There was a little delay, but it was soon over and they were shaking hands warmly all around.

"It seems so delightful to go off on another trip!" said Dora, to Dick. "I know I am going to enjoy it very much!"

"And I know I am going to enjoy it, too—with you along," answered Dick, with a smile which spoke volumes.

"Mother is quite excited—thinking she is going on a treasure hunt," went on Dora. "But I think a few days' rest on shipboard will quiet her nerves."

"I hope for your sake, Dora, our hunt proves successful," added Dick, gallantly.

"I have always wanted to go to the West Indies," said Nellie Lanning to Tom. "I want to pick some ripe bananas and cocoanuts right from the trees."

"Yes, and ripe oranges," put in Grace. "Won't it be jolly?" she added, turning to Sam.

"Too jolly for anything!" murmured Sam, and then he gave Grace's arm a little squeeze and led her through the crowd to where a carriage was in waiting.

There were trunks to be looked after, but the checks for these were turned over to Aleck, and the colored man saw to it that all the baggage was properly transferred to the steam yacht.

It was with not a little pride that the boys took the Stanhopes and the Lanings aboard the *Rainbow*, for, although they did not own the elegant craft it was something to even have her under charter. Mr. Rover met the newcomers at the gangplank and made them welcome.

"Oh, but isn't this just too lovely for anything!" cried Dora, as she surveyed the double stateroom assigned to her and her mother. "And look at the fine bunch of roses on the stand!" She looked at Dick. "This is some of your doings, isn't it?"

"Yes."

"Thank you very much! But you must have one," and the girl promptly pinned one of the largest in his buttonhole.

"This is more than comfortable," said Mrs. Stanhope, with a sigh of satisfaction. And then she sank down in an easy chair to rest, for the long journey from Cedarville had greatly fatigued her.

In the meantime the other boys had taken the Lanings to another double stateroom, equally luxurious. Here a vase held a big bunch of carnations, the gift of Tom and Sam combined. Nellie and Grace and their mother were much pleased and said so.

"Tom, I could almost hug you for this!" cried Nellie, in a low voice.

"Well, nobody is stopping you," he added promptly.

"All right, I will—on your next birthday," cried Nellie, not to be caught. "But really, I'm a thousand times obliged to you."

"This is like a room in a fairies' palace!" exclaimed Grace. "I know when I go to sleep I'll dream of fairies and rainbows, and pots of gold—"

"The gold we want to unearth," broke in Sam. "Just dream where that is located and then tell us of it."

"Oh, you'll be sure to find that."

"How do you know."

"Oh, you never fail in anything," and Grace gave him a sunny smile.

"I don't know about that, Grace. This is going to be no easy task."

"Oh, I know that, Sam, but you'll win in the end, I know you will."

"I trust we do—for your sake as much as for the others. You know if it is found a good share of the treasure goes to your mother."

"Yes, and that will be awfully nice."

"Maybe, if you get all that money, you won't notice poor me."

"Poor you? Why, you'll have a great deal more than we'll have anyway. You are rich already."

"Well, if you get the money you won't forget me, will you?" persisted Sam.

"What a queer boy you are, Sam! Forget you! Well, just try me with the money and see!" she added, and gave him one of her warmest smiles. Then she danced off to look at the rest of the steam yacht, and the youngest Rover followed her.

CHAPTER XII.
SOMETHING ABOUT FIRECRACKERS

All was in readiness for departure but one thing, and that was the most important of all. Bahama Bill had not put in an appearance and was not expected until the evening of the Fourth of July.

"We shall have to remain over the Fourth after all," said Anderson Rover. "But I imagine that will suit you boys, for you can stay in the city and have some fun."

It did suit all the young folks, and they immediately planned a fine automobile tour for the afternoon, hiring two autos large enough to accommodate all of the girls and boys. The morning was spent in and around the yacht, where Tom and some of the others amused themselves by shooting off their pistols and some firecrackers. Tom had purchased some things for the Fourth the day previous and he had one package which he was careful to keep out of sight.

"I am going to have a barrel of fun with the girls," he said to his brothers. "But don't tell anybody about it."

"What is it?" asked his younger brother.

"Wait and see."

It had been arranged that the whole party should have an early lunch, so that they might start on the automobile ride by one o'clock. Aleck was in charge of the dining room of the yacht and he had spread himself in trimming it with red, white and blue streamers and small flags.

"Oh, how lovely!" cried Dora, as she came in and sat down. "I declare, Aleck, you deserve a great deal of credit." And she gave the colored man a smile which pleased him immensely.

"Where is Tom?" asked Mr. Rover, after all the others were seated.

"I ton't know," answered Hans. "Tidn't he know ve vos to eat a leetle early to tay?"

"He's coming," answered Sam.

Just then Tom came into the dining room holding something in his hand covered with a long paper bag. From under the bag smoke was curling.

"In honor of the Fourth of July!" cried the fun-loving Rover and placed the object upright in the center of the long table. Then he took off the bag with a flourish. There was revealed a big cannon cracker, fully a foot and a half high and several inches in diameter. The fuse was spluttering away at a great rate.

"Tom!" Yelled Mr. Rover in alarm. "Throw that thing out!"

"We'll be blown to pieces!" yelled Fred.

"That's too big to shoot off indoors," added songbird, preparing to run.

"Ve peen knocked to bieces!" groaned Hans, and slid under the table out of sight.

The ladies shrieked and so did the girls. Mrs. Stanhope looked ready to faint, but Tom whispered hastily into her ear and she recovered. Mr. Rover wanted to throw the cannon cracker through a window, but Tom held him back.

The long fuse continued to splutter and all watched it as if fascinated, and the girls put their hands to their ears in anticipation of a fearful explosion. Then came a tiny flash, a strange clicking, and off flew the top of the cannon cracker, sending a shower of confetti of various colors in all directions.

"Oh!" shrieked the girls, and then everybody but Hans set up a laugh. The German youth looked suspiciously out from under the table.

"Vot's der madder—did he go off?" he questioned.

"Yes, he did, Hans," answered Grace. "It was nothing but a cracker full of colored paper instead of powder."

"Is dot so?" Hans got up and looked around. "Vell, I neffer! Looks like ve got a colored snowstorm alretty, hey?" And this caused a roar. It certainly did look like a "colored snowstorm," for the confetti was everywhere, on the table, on their heads and over their clothing. Now it was over everybody was highly amused, even Mrs. Stanhope laughing heartily. As for Aleck, he roared so loudly he could be heard a block up the docks.

"Dat's jess like Massa Tom!" he cried. "I suspicioned he'd be up to somet'ing afo' de day was up. Yo' can't keep him down no mo' dan yo' kin keep a jack rabbit from hoppin', no, sah!"

"It certainly looked like the real thing," was Mr. Rover's comment. "Had it been—"

"I'd never have brought it in here," finished Tom. "I'm sorry if I frightened anybody," he added, looking at Mrs. Stanhope and Mrs. Laning.

"We'll forgive you, Tom," answered Mrs. Stanhope, and Mrs. Laning said she would, provided he wouldn't scare them again that holiday.

After that, the confetti on the table was cleared away and they ate their lunch amid a constant cracking of jokes and bright sayings. Songbird woke up and recited some verses he said he had composed the night before, while lying awake in his berth. Some of these ran in this fashion:

"This is the day I love the best—
The day the small boy knows no rest,—
The day when all our banners soar,
The day when all our cannons roar,
The day when all are free from care,
And shouts and music fill the air!"

"Good for Songbird!" cried Sam.

"Go on, please!" came from the girls, and the poet of Putnam Hall continued:

"I love this land of liberty
From mountains down to flowing sea,
I love its cities and its plains,
Its valleys and its rocky chains,
I'm glad to know that we are free,
And so forever may we be!"

"Hurrah, Songbird, you ought to have that put to music," cried Dick.

"Maybe I will, some day," answered the would-be poet modestly.

"I dink I make some boetry up, too," remarked Hans, after several minutes of serious thought on his part. "Chust you listen vonce!" And he began:

"Dis is der day ven crackers bust
Und fill der air mid bowder tust,
Und ven you shoots your bistol off,
You make a smokes vot makes you cough.
A rocket goes up in der sky—
Der sthick vos hit you in der eye!"

"Three cheers for Hans!" shouted Tom, clapping the German lad on the back. "For real, first class A, No. 1, first chop poetry that can't be beat." And then as the others screamed with laughter Tom went on:

"A little boy,
A can of powder,
A scratch, a flash—
He's gone to chowder!"

"Oh, Tom, what horrible poetry!" cried Nellie, as she shivered.

"Well, I couldn't help it," he said. "I had to say something or—or bust! Perhaps this will suit you better," and he continued:

"A little boy,
A great big gun,
A father yelling
On the run.
The trigger falls,
There is a roar.
The father halts—
The danger's o'er."

"Tom, you're positively the worst boy ever!" said Nellie, but the way she spoke told she meant just the opposite.

"I tell you vot ve vos do, Tom," suggested Hans. "Ve vos form a boetry association alretty, hey? Songpirt can be der bresident."

"What will you be, secretary?" asked Fred.

"No, I vos peen treasurer," answered Hans.

"Hans wants the money," put in Dick.

"Dot's it," answered the German youth calmly. "Ven dem udder fellers makes up pad verses I vos fine dem a tollar, und ven I gits enough tollars I skip me to Canada or Mexigo, hey?" And he said this so comically everybody had to laugh.

The automobiles had been ordered down to the dock and were already in waiting. Each was in charge of a chauffeur, and soon the boys and girls went ashore and piled in. Dick and Dora, Sam and Grace, and Fred got in the first turnout and the others in the second.

"Now do not go too far," said Mrs. Stanhope, "and be sure and keep on roads that are safe."

"And do not stay out later than ten o'clock this evening," added Mrs. Laning.

"Oh, we'll be back safe and sound and on time," cried Dick. "So don't worry about us."

"Those are both powerful machines," was Mr. Rover's comment. "Be careful that you don't exceed the speed limits, or you may be arrested."

"Providing they catch us," answered Tom, with a grin.

It had been decided that they should go out into the country by the way of Germantown, and soon they were bowling along in fine fashion over the smooth city pavement. Here and there they met crowds shooting off pistols and firecrackers.

"It is good we haven't horses," said Sam. "This racket might cause them to run away."

"That is where the automobilist has the advantage over a horse driver, Sam," answered his big brother. "But I must say, some of the young fellows on the street are rather careless."

Scarcely had Dick spoken when the big machine rounded a corner and speeded through a crowd of what were evidently factory hands. They were shooting off pistols and firecrackers and raised a great din. Then one ugly looking young fellow lighted a firecracker and sent it toward the automobile. It landed directly in Dora's lap.

"Oh!" screamed Dora, and tried to draw away.

As quick as a flash Dick leaned forward and caught up the firecracker. As he threw it out of the automobile it exploded close by.

"Do that again, and I'll come back at you!" shouted the elder Rover, and shook his fist at the fellow in the street.

"Dick, did it hurt you?" asked Dora, anxiously.

"Oh, it burst my little finger a trifle, that's all," was the reply. The finger smarted quite some, but Dick did not want to show it.

"We ought to go back and punch his head," was Sam's comment.

"Wonder if they'll try that game on the other auto," said Fred, as he arose to look back.

He saw the street rough throw a lighted firecracker at the other machine. It landed on the floor of the tonneau, but like a flash Tom was after it. The fun-loving Rover held it up, took aim, and sent it straight at the fellow who had first launched it. Bang! went the firecracker, right close to the rough's left ear. He set up a howl of pain, for he had been burnt enough to make it smart well.

"There, he's paid back," said Fred, and then the two automobiles passed on, leaving the roughs in the distance.

CHAPTER XIII.
A WILD AUTOMOBILE RIDE

"This is glorious!"

"It certainly could not be finer, Dick."

"Some day, Dora, I am going to take you for a long ride," went on Dick. "I mean some day after we get home with that treasure," he added, in a lower tone, so that the chauffeur might not hear.

"That's a long time off, Dick."

"Perhaps not so long."

"And what are you going to do after this hunt is over?"

"Go to college, I guess. It is not yet fully decided, for we don't know what college to go to."

"I hope—" Dora broke off short.

"What, Dora."

"Oh, I was just thinking. Mamma thinks that I might go to college. If I went it would be nice if we went to two places that were near each other."

"Nice? It would be the best ever!" cried Dick, enthusiastically.

They were running along a country road a good many miles from Philadelphia. All the noise of the city had been left behind and it was as calm and peaceful as one would wish. The second machine was only a short distance behind the first, and each was making not less than thirty miles per hour.

"Do you know, some day I am going to make a regular tour in an auto," remarked Sam. "I am sure a fellow could have lots of fun."

"You can have this machine any time you want to," said the chauffeur, who had taken greatly to, the party.

"We'll remember," answered Dick, indifferently. He did not particularly fancy the fellow, for he was rather familiar and his breath smelt of liquor. Twice he had talked of stopping at road houses, but Dick had told him to go on, fearful that he might drink too much.

A hill was before the automobiles, but both machines climbed it without an effort. From the top of the hill a fine view was to be obtained, and here a hotel had been located, and this displayed a sign which interested the boys and girls very much:

ICE CREAM.
SODA WATER. ROOT BEER.
BEST CANDY.

"Let us stop for some ice cream," suggested Songbird. And he yelled to those in the automobile ahead.

All of the girls loved ice cream, so despite Dick's anxiety over his chauffeur, a stop was made, and the boys and girls filed into the hotel for the treat. Dick lingered behind to speak to both of the machine drivers, for he saw that the second man was of the same "thirsty" type as the other.

"Do you smoke?" he asked.

"Sure," was the reply from both.

"Then here is a quarter with which you can buy some cigars. And please remember, no drinking," he added, significantly.

"Can't a fellow have a drink if he wants it?" demanded the chauffeur of the first car.

"Not while you have my party out," was Dick's reply.

"Well, a fellow gets thirsty, driving a car in this dust," grumbled the second chauffeur.

"If you are thirsty, there is plenty of water handy and root beer and soda water, too. I meant liquor when I spoke."

"Oh, we'll keep straight enough, don't you worry," said the first chauffeur, and then both of them turned away to a side entrance of the hotel.

Dick was much worried, but he did not let the rest see it. He joined the crowd in the ice cream pavillion attached to the hotel, and there they spent an hour, eating ice cream, water ices, and cake. Then some of the lads went off and got several boxes of bonbons and chocolates to take along on the rest of the trip.

When they went out to the two automobiles the chauffeurs were missing. A man was trimming a hedge nearby and Dick asked him if he had seen the pair.

"Must be over to the barroom," said the gardener. "That Hellig loves his liquor, and Snall likes a glass, too."

"Was Hellig the driver of this first car?"

"Yes, and Snall ran the second."

Just then Tom came up, having placed Nellie in the second car.

"What's the trouble, Dick?" he questioned.

"I am afraid both our men have gone off to drink. This man says they both love their liquor."

"They do, and both of 'em have been locked up for reckless driving but don't say I told you," said the gardener.

"Humph! This is serious," murmured Tom. "I don't like to trust a chauffeur who drinks."

"Come with me," said his brother, in a low tone. "Just wait for us," he shouted to the others, who were now in the two cars.

He walked behind the ice cream pavillion, Tom at his side, and then the pair reached a side door, connecting with the hotel barroom. They looked in and at a small table saw the two chauffeurs drinking liquor from a bottle set before them. Both were rather noisy and had evidently been imbibing freely.

"I won't let no boy run me and tell me what I shall take," they heard Hellig say thickly.

"I'll drink what I please and when I please," answered Snall. "Let us have another, Nat."

"Sure."

"This is the worst ever!" murmured Tom. "They are in no fit condition to run the cars. I wouldn't trust my neck with either of them."

"And I am not going to trust the lives of the girls in their care," answered Dick, firmly.

"What are you going to do?"

"I don't know yet. But one thing is settled—, they shan't take us back."

"I think I could run one car—if we didn't go too fast," suggested Tom, who had run several machines at various times in his lively career.

"I could run the other."

"Then let us do it, Dick. Those fellows don't own the cars, and we didn't hire from them, we hired from the owner of the garage. I guess we have a right to run them under the circumstances."

The two boys walked back to the automobiles. All of the others were now anxious to know what was wrong and they had to give the particulars.

"Oh, Dick, you must not let them run the cars!" cried Grace, turning pale.

"I'd rather have you and Tom run them ten times over," declared Dora.

While the party was talking the two chauffeurs came from the hotel and walked unsteadily towards the automobiles. Their faces were red and their eyes blinked unsteadily.

"Stop!" called Dick, when they were some distance away, and the gardener and some guests of the hotel gathered around to see what was the matter.

"What yer want?" growled Hellig, thickly.

"We are going to leave you both here and run the cars ourselves," answered Dick, coldly. "You are not fit to run them."

"What's the reason we ain't?" mumbled Snall. He could hardly speak.

"You've been drinking too much—that's the reason."

"Humph!"

"We are going to run them machines an' don't you forgit it," mumbled Hellig, and lurched forward.

"Don't you ride with those intoxicated fellows," said one of the hotel guests.

"We don't intend to," answered Dick. "All ready, Tom?" he called out.

"Yes."

"Then go ahead. I'll catch up to you."

82 | The Rover Boys On Treasure Isle or The Strange Cruise of the Steam Yacht.

"Hi, you stop!" screamed Snall, as one of the automobiles began to move off down the road. But Tom paid no attention to him.

Running swiftly, Dick reached the other car and hopped up to the chauffeur's seat. He had watched the driver operate the car and knew exactly what to do. He soon had the engine running and then he threw in the speed clutch just as Hellig lurched up.

"You mustn't ran away with that machine!" he roared.

"Keep away!" cried Sam, and leaning out of the car he gave the chauffeur a shove that sent him flat on his back in the dust of the road. Then the car moved off. As those in the automobile looked back they saw Hellig arise and shake his fist after them and Snall waved his arms wildly.

"We'll hear from them again, I suppose," said Sam.

"And they'll hear from me," answered Dick. "and the fellow who sent them out to run the cars for us will hear from me, too," he added.

Tom was quite a distance ahead, but they soon caught up to his car. By this time they were out of sight and hearing of the hotel, and going down the other side of the hill they had come up.

"If you wish, you can take the lead," said the fun-loving Rover to his older brother. "I don't know a thing about these roads."

"We'll have to trust to luck and the signboards," returned Dick.

"It will be all right if only you don't get on some road that is impassible," put in Fred.

"And get stuck thirty miles from nowhere," added Songbird.

"You stick to dem roads vot haf stones on de got," said Hans wisely. "Ton't you vos, drust der car to der tirt roads, no!"

"I shall follow Hans' advice and stick to the good roads," said Dick. "I think the signboards will help us to get back to Philadelphia sooner or later."

They sped down the hill and there found the road turned to the left and crossed a small stream. Then they reached a corner with several signboards.

"Hurrah! that's the way to Philly!" cried Sam.

"But it doesn't say how many miles," protested Grace.

"Never mind, we are bound to get there before dark, and that is all we care," came from Nellie.

In the exhilaration of running the cars, Dick and Tom soon forgot about the trouble with the chauffeurs. It was great sport, and as soon as Dick "got the hang of it," as he said, he let the speed out, notch by notch. His car ran a trifle more easily than did the other and before long he was a good half mile ahead of that run by Tom. Those in the rear shouted for him to slow down, but the wind prevented him from hearing their calls.

"This is something like, isn't it?" said Dick to Dora, who was beside him.

"Oh, it is splendid!" she replied enthusiastically. "I feel as if I could go on riding forever!"

"An auto certainly beats a team all to bits, if the road is good."

They passed up another hill, and then through a patch of woods. Then they made a sharp turn, and the car began to descend over a road that was filled with loose stones.

"Say, Dick, you'd better slow up," cautioned Sam, as the machine gave a quick lurch over a stone. "This road isn't as smooth as it was."

"I know it."

"I saw a road to our right," said Grace. "Perhaps we should have taken that."

There was no time to say more, for the automobile was jouncing over the stones in too lively a manner. Alarmed, Dick, who had already shut off the power, applied the brake, but he was not used to this and he jammed it fast so it did not altogether prevent the car from advancing.

"Oh, we must stop!" screamed Dora, a moment later. "Look ahead!"

Dick did so, and his heart gave a leap of fear. Below them the stony road was narrow, and on one side was a rocky gully and on the other some thick bushes. In the roadway was a farmer with a large farm wagon filled with lime. Should they hit the turnout below somebody would surely be hurt and perhaps killed.

CHAPTER XIV.
WHAT A ROMAN CANDLE DID

It was a time for quick action, and it was a lucky thing that Dick Rover had been in perilous positions before and knew enough not to lose his presence of mind. As the others in the automobile arose to leap out he called to them:

"Sit down! Don't jump! I'll look out for things!"

Then, even as he spoke, Dick turned the steering wheel and sent the big machine crashing into the bushes to one side of the roadway. He chose a spot that was comparatively level, and in five seconds they came to a halt just in front of half a dozen trees.

"We must take care of Tom's machine!" cried Sam, and leaped over the back of the automobile. The machine had cut down the bushes, so the path was clear and he ran with might and main to the roadway. At the top of the hill was the second car, coming along at a good speed.

"Stop! stop!" he yelled, frantically, and waved his arms in the air.

Tom saw the movement and knew at once something was wrong. He threw off the power and applied the emergency brake and the automobile just passed Sam and no more.

"What's the matter?" came from everyone in the second car.

"That's what's the matter," answered Sam, pointing to the foot of the rocky hill. "That wagon—Well, I declare!"

The youngest Rover stared and well he might, for the farmer's turnout with the load of lime had disappeared from view. The farmer had turned into a field at the bottom of the hill just as Dick turned his car into the bushes.

"I don't see anything," said Nellie. And then Sam had to explain and point out the situation of the first car.

"I guess I can get down the hill well enough," said Tom. "But this appears to be a poor road. We ought to try to find something better."

All those in the second car got out and walked to that which was stalled in the bushes. They found Dick and Fred walking around the machine trying to learn if any damage had been done.

"We might have kept right on," said Sam, and explained why.

"Well, we are here, and now comes the problem of getting back on the road," said the eldest Rover. "I don't think I can back very well in here."

"Better make a turn on the down grade," suggested Sam. "We can cut down some of the big bushes that are in the way, and fill up some of the holes with stones."

It was decided to do this, and all of the boys took off their coats and went to work. Soon they had a fairly clear path, and after backing away a few feet from the trees, Dick turned downward in a semi circle, and got out once more on the road. This time he was mindful to use the brake with care, and consequently he gained the bottom of the stony hill without further mishap, and the second machine came after him.

"There is that farmer," said Songbird. "Why not ask him about the roads?"

"I will," said Dick, and stalked into the field.

"This ain't no good road to Philadelphia," said the farmer, when questioned. "Better go back up the hill and take the road on the right."

"We can't get back very well."

"Then you had better go along this road and take the first turn to the left and after that the next turn to the right. You'll have about three miles o' poor roads, but then you'll be all right, but the distance to the city is six miles longer."

There was no help for it and they went on, over dirt roads which were anything but good. They had to go slowly, and Tom kept the second car far to the rear, to escape the thick dust sent up by the leading machine.

"This isn't so fine," declared Dick, with a grimace at Dora. "I am sorry we took that false turn at the top of the hill."

"Oh, we'll have to take the bitter with the sweet," answered the girl, lightly.

"I shan't mind it if you don't, Dora."

"Don't worry, Dick, I am not minding it a bit. I am only glad we got rid of that intoxicated chauffeur. He might have gotten us into far more trouble than this."

Inside of an hour they found themselves on a good stone road and reached a signboard put up by the automobile association, telling the exact distance to Philadelphia. This set them at ease mentally, and they started off at a speed of twenty miles an hour. Tom wanted to "let her out," as he put it, but Nellie demurred and so he kept to the rear as before.

"But some day I am going to have a machine of my own," said he, "and it is going to do some speeding, I can tell you that."

"Yah, and der first dings you know, Dom, you vos ub a dree odder you sphlit a rock insides owid," warned Hans. "Ven I ride so fast like dot I valk, I pet you!"

It was dark long before the city was reached and they had to stop to light the lamps, and they also had to fix the batteries of the second car. Fred, who was getting hungry, suggested they stop somewhere for something to eat, but the girls demurred.

"Wait until the ride is ended," said Dora. "Then we can take our time over supper."

As night came on they saw fireworks displayed here and there and enjoyed the sights greatly.

"I've got some fireworks on the yacht," said Tom. "I reckon I'll be rather late setting them off."

While they were yet three miles from the river they stopped at a drug store and there Dick telephoned to the owner of the machines, explaining matters, and asking the man to send down to the dock for the cars.

"He's pretty angry," said Dick, as he leaped into the automobile again. "He says we had no right to run off with the cars."

"Well, he had no right to send us off with those awful chauffeurs," answered Dora.

"Oh, I'm not afraid of anything he'll do," answered Dick.

Nevertheless, he was a bit anxious as he reached the dock, and he lost no time in sending the girls to the yacht with Songbird, and he asked his chum to send Mr. Rover ashore.

A minute later a light runabout spun up and a tall, thin man, with a sour face, leaped out and strode up to the two machines.

"Who hired these machines, I want to know?" he demanded. "I did," answered Dick boldly. "Are you the manager of the garage?"

"I am, and I want to know by what right you've been running the cars without the regular drivers?"

"We wanted to get back to the city and the chauffeurs were in no condition to bring us back," put in Tom.

"What have you to do with it, young man?"

"I drove one car and my brother here drove the other. We didn't hurt the machines and you ought to be glad we brought them back in good condition."

"Humph! You hadn't any license to run them."

"We took the liberty of doing so," said Dick. "If you want to get angry about it, I'll get angry myself. You had no right to place those cars in the hands of unreliable men. You risked our lives by so doing."

"Those men are reliable enough. One of them telephoned to me you had run away with the autos."

"The folks at the Dardell Hotel will tell you how reliable they were. I warned them not to drink, but they did, and they were in no condition to run any automobile."

"I don't allow just anybody to run my machines," stormed the man. "They are expensive pieces of property."

"Well, they are not worth as much as our necks, not by a good deal," said Tom.

"Don't you get impudent, young fellow!"

"He is not impudent," said Dick. "Your machines are all right—we didn't hurt them in the least. But I can tell you one thing," he proceeded earnestly. "We don't propose to pay for the hire of the chauffeurs."

"That's the talk," broke in Fred. "Pay him for the use of the cars only."

"You'll pay the whole bill!" growled the automobile owner.

"Not a cent more than the hire of the two cars," said Tom

The man began to storm, and threatened to have them locked up for running the cars without a license. But in the end he accepted the money Dick offered him.

"Maybe you haven't heard the end of this," he muttered.

"If you make trouble, perhaps I'll do the same," answered Dick, and then he and the others went aboard the yacht, where a late supper awaited them. Mr. Rover had heard of the unreliable chauffeurs and he was even more indignant than his sons.

"I don't think that owner will show himself again," he said. "If he does I'll take care of him." The man was never heard of; and that ended the affair.

"We had a splendid time anyway," declared Grace, and the other girls agreed with her.

Tom had not forgotten about his fireworks, and after supper he invited the crowd to the deck and gave them quite an exhibition.

"Here, Hans, you can set off this Roman candle," he said, presently. "Show the ladies how nicely you can do it. But take off your coat and roll up your shirt sleeve before you begin," he added, with a dig into Sam's ribs, which meant, "watch for fun."

Quite innocently the German lad took off his coat and rolled his shirt sleeve up over his elbow. Then he took the big Roman candle and lit it.

"Now swing it around lively," cried Tom, and Hans began to describe little circles with the Roman candle. Soon the sparks began to pour forth, and not a few came down on the bare wrist and forearm.

"Ouch! ouch!" yelled Hans, dancing around. "Ach du meine zeit! Say, somepody sthop dot! I vos purn mineselluf ub alretty!"

"Swing it around quicker!" cried Dick.

"Turn it in the shape of a figure eight!" suggested Fred.

"Loop the loop with it," came from Sam.

Around and around went the Roman candle and then bang! out shot a ball, hitting one of the masts of the steam yacht. Then bang! went another ball, hitting the top of the cabin.

"Hold it up straighter, Hans!" said Songbird. "Don't shoot somebody."

"If I hold him ub I burn mineselluf worser!" groaned the German youth.

"Here, you dake him, Sam, I got enough."

"No, no, Hans, I won't deprive you of the pleasure of shooting it off," answered the youngest Rover, and skipped out of the way.

One after another the balls, red, white and blue, poured from the Roman candle. It was a pretty sight, but Hans' aim was more than bad, and one hit the bow and another the stern, while a third whizzed past Dick's ear. In the meantime Hans was hopping around like a madman, trying to keep the sparks from his skin.

"Throw it overboard!" cried Mr. Rover, who was enjoying the fun, but who was afraid somebody might get a fire ball in the face.

"Only a few more balls left," said Tom. "Hans, try to hit the top of the mast don't point it downward."

The German youth was too excited to listen to the advice. He continued to dance around. Bang! went another ball and entered the cabin of the steam yacht. Bang! came the final one and that too disappeared into the interior of the craft. Then the Roman candle went out, and Hans breathed a sigh of relief.

"I vos glat dot is ofer," he said. "No more firevorks for me, not on your kollarbuttons, no!"

"I hope they didn't do any damage in the cabin—" began Mrs. Stanhope anxiously, when there came a cry from Aleck Pop.

"Stop dat fire from comin' down!" yelled the colored man. "De hull cabin's in a blaze!"

CHAPTER XV.
THE SAILING OF THE STEAM YACHT

The announcement made by Aleck Pop filled all on board the steam yacht with consternation, and while Hans still nursed his arm and wrist the other boys, with Anderson Rover and Captain Barforth, rushed down the companionway.

A glance showed them what was the matter. One of the balls of fire had struck a curtain and ignited the flimsy material. The fire was now dropping down on some fireworks Tom had left on a chair. Just as they entered a pinwheel, lying flat, began to fizz, sending a shower of sparks across the other pieces.

"Quick! out with that stuff!" cried Anderson Rover and sent the pinwheel flying into a corner with his hand. Then he stepped on it, putting out the fire.

In the meantime, Dick and Sam pulled down the burning curtain and stamped on that. The others scattered the fireworks and saw to it that not a spark remained in the cabin.

"A close call!" murmured Captain Barforth, when the excitement was over. "It is lucky we got down here so soon."

"I was thinkin' de hull ship was gwine ter bust up!" said Aleck, with a shiver. "Dis chile knows jess how quick fireworks kin go off. I see a big combustication of dem one summer in a hotel where I was waiting. Da had to call de fire department to put dem out an' da shot out moah dan a dozen winders, too!"

"We had a similar trouble, when the yacht club had a celebration," said the captain. "A Japanese lantern dropped on some rockets and set them off. The rockets flew in all directions and one struck a deck hand in the arm and he had to go to the hospital to be treated. We have had a lucky escape."

The accident put a damper on more celebrating, and Tom was requested to store away what remained of the fireworks. Little did he dream of how useful those fireworks were to become in the future.

Early on the following morning Bahama Bill, presented himself. The boys had been told how he looked, yet they had all they could do to keep from smiling when he presented himself. He was a short, thickset man, with broad shoulders, and legs which were very much bowed. He wore his reddish hair long and also sported a thick beard. He had a squint in one eye which, as Sam said, "gave him the appearance of looking continually over his shoulder. When he talked his voice was an alternate squeak and rumble.

"Well, of all the odd fellows I ever met he is the limit," was Tom's comment. "Why, he'd do for a comic valentine!"

"I almost had to laugh in his face," said Sam. "Even now I can't look at him without grinning."

"He's a character," was Dick's opinion. "You'll never get tired with that chap around," and in this surmise he was correct, for Bahama Bill was as full of sea yarns as some fish are full of bones, and he was willing to talk as long as anybody would listen to him.

"Very much pleased to know ye all," said he with a profound bow to the ladies. "Ain't seen such a nice crowd since I sailed on the Mary Elizabeth, up the coast o' Maine, jest fourteen years ago. At that time we had on board Captain Rigger's wife, his mother in law, his two sisters, his brother's wife, his aunt and—"

"Never mind the Rigger family just now, Camel,"
interrupted Mr. Rover.
"What I want to know is, are you ready to sail?"

"Aye, aye! that I am, and I don't care if it's a for two months or two years. Once when I sailed on the Sunflower the captain said we'd be out a month, and we struck a storm and drifted almost over to the coast a' Africy. The water ran low, and—"

"Well, if you are ready to sail, we'll start without further delay," interrupted Anderson Rover, and gave the necessary orders to Captain Barforth.

"Good bye to home!" cried Dick, and took off his cap. "When we return may we have the treasure safely stowed away in the hold or the cabin!"

"So say we all of us!" sang out Tom.

Steam was already up and a cloud of smoke was pouring from the funnel of the steam yacht. The lines were cast off, and a few minutes later the vessel was on her voyage down the Delaware River to the bay.

"You are sure we have everything necessary for this trip?" asked Mr. Rover, of the captain.

"Yes, Mr. Rover; I even brought along some picks and shovels," answered the master of the steam yacht, and smiled faintly. He had little faith in the treasure hunt being successful, but he thought the trip down among the West Indies would be well worth taking.

It was a beautiful day, with just sufficient breeze blowing to cool the July air. While they were steaming down the river the girls and ladies, and some of the boys, sat on the forward deck taking in the various sights which presented themselves. There were numerous tugs and sailing craft, and now and then a big tramp steamer or regular liner, for Philadelphia has a large commerce with the entire world.

"It hardly seems possible that the treasure hunt has really begun," said Dora to Dick.

"Well, it won't actually begin until we are down about where Treasure Isle is located," was the reply. "We have quite a few days' sailing before that time comes."

"I hope it remains clear, Dick."

"I am afraid it won't, Dora; there are always more or less storms among the West Indies."

"I have heard they sometimes have terrible hurricanes," came from Grace. "I read of one hurricane which flooded some small islands completely."

"Grace is trying to scare us!" cried Nellie.

"Well, islands have been swept by hurricanes," said Sam, coming to the rescue of his dearest girl friend. "But let us hope we escape all heavy storms."

"A steam yacht is not as bad off as a sailing vessel," said Dick. "If necessary, we can run away from a heavy storm. In a high wind it's a sailing ship that catches it."

By nightfall they had passed out of Delaware Bay into the Atlantic Ocean, and then the course was changed to almost due south. As soon as they got out on the long swells the *Rainbow* commenced to toss and pitch considerably.

"Now you can sing a life on the ocean wave!" cried Dick to Songbird. "How does this suit you?"

"Elegant!" was the reply, and then the would-be poet began to warble:

"I love the rolling ocean
With all its strange commotion
And all the washing wavelets that hit us on the side;
I love to hear the dashing
Of the waves and see the splashing
Of the foam that chums around us as on we glide!"

"Gee Christopher!" cried Sam. "Say, Songbird, that rhyme is enough to make one dizzy!"

"I dink dot boetry vos make me tizzy already," came from Hans, as he sat down on a nearby chair, his face growing suddenly pale.

"Hullo, Hans is sick!" cried Tom. "Hans, I thought you had better sea legs than that."

"I vosn't sick at all, Dom, only vell, der ship looks like be vos going to dake a summersaults already kvick!"

"You're seasick," said Sam. "Better go to your stateroom and lie down."

"I ton't vos going to get seasick," protested the German youth.

"Think of Hansy getting seasick!" cried Fred. "That's the best yet!" And he laughed heartily. "Shall I hold your head for you?" he asked, with a grin.

"I guess it vos der fireworks yesterday done him," said Hans weakly, and staggered off to the cabin.

"That's kind of rough to twit him, Fred," remarked Dick.

"Oh, I only meant it in fun."

"Maybe you'll get seasick yourself."

"Not much! If I do, I have a remedy in my trunk, that I brought from home."

"You'd better give the remedy to Hans."

"I will."

Fred went below and got the bottle of medicine from his dress suit case. As he did this his own head began to swim around, much to his alarm.

"Here, Hans, is a dose for you," he said, entering the stateroom, where the German youth was rolling around on the berth.

"Vot ist it for?" groaned the sufferer.

"Seasickness."

"Den gif it to me kvick! Gif me apout two quarts!"

"It says take a tablespoonful," said Fred, reading the label with difficulty. "Here you are."

He administered the medicine, which Hans took without a murmur, although it was very bitter. Then he tried to take a dose himself, but his stomach suddenly "went back on him," and he let the bottle fall with a crash to the floor.

"Oh, my! you vos lose all dot goot medicine!" cried Hans, in alarm.

"I—I know it," groaned Fred. "And I—er—I need it so much!"

"Vot, you seasick, too? Ha, ha! Dot's vot you gits for boking fun at me, yah!" And Hans smiled in spite of his anguish.

It was certainly poetic justice that Fred should get seasick and that the malady should affect him far more seriously than it did Hans. The medicine given to the German lad made him feel better in less than an hour, while poor Fred suffered until noon of the next day. None of the other boys were affected. The ladies and the girls felt rather dizzy, and Mrs. Stanhope had to lie down until the next forenoon, but by the evening of the next day all were around as before, and then seasickness became a thing of the past.

"Can't tell nuthin' about that seasickness," said Bahama Bill, to Tom, after hearing how ill Fred was. "I remember onct I took a voyage to Rio, in South America. We had a cap'n as had sailed the sea for forty years an' a mate who had been across the ocean sixteen times. Well, sir, sure as I'm here we struck some thick weather with the Johnny Jackson tumblin' an' tossin' good, and the cap'n an' the mate took seasick an' was sick near the hull trip. Then the second mate got down, an' the bosun, an' then the cook, an—"

"The cabin boy—" suggested Tom.

"No, we didn't have any cabin boy. Next—"

"Maybe the second fireman caught it."

"No, this was a bark an' we didn't have no second fireman, nor fust, neither. Next—"

"Maybe the cat, or don't cats get seasick?"

"The cat. Why, mate—"

"I see some cats get sick, but that may not be seasick, even though you can see the sickness," went on Tom, soberly.

"I don't know as we had a cat on board. But as I was sayin', next—"

"Oh, I know what you are driving at, Bill. Next the steersman got down with the mumps, then you took the shingles, and another sailor got lumbago, while the third mate had to crawl around with a boil on his foot as large as a cabbage. I heard about that affair—read about it in the last monthly number of the Gasman's Gazette—how the ship had to sail itself for four weeks and how the wind blew it right into port and how not even a shoestring was lost overboard. It was really wonderful and I am thankful you reminded me of it." And then Tom walked off, leaving Bahama Bill staring after him in dumb amazement. The old tar realized dimly that for once he had met his match at yarn spinning, and it was several days before he attempted to tell any more of his outrageous stories.

CHAPTER XVI.
A ROW ON SHIPBOARD

"Do you know, I think we are going on the wildest kind of a goose chase," said Tom, the next day, to his two brothers.

"Why?" questioned Sam.

"Because we are depending, in large part, on what Bahama Bill has to tell, he's the worst yarn spinner I ever ran across."

"It's true that he is a yam spinner," said Dick, "but behind it all father says he tells a pretty straight story of how the treasure was stolen and secreted on Treasure Isle."

"I want to see the island, and the treasure, too, before I'll believe one quarter of what that sailor says," replied Tom.

"Well, we'll soon know the truth of the matter," came from Sam. "If this good weather continues we ought to get to where we are going inside of ten days. Of course, if we are held up by fogs or storms it will take longer."

The boys, and the girls, too, for the matter of that, were greatly interested in the elegant steam yacht, and they took great pleasure in visiting every part of the vessel from bow to stem. Captain Barforth did all in his power to make all on board the *Rainbow* feel at home and whenever the boys visited the engine room they were met with a smile from Frank Norton.

But if they had friends on board there were also some persons they did not like. The first mate, whose name was Asa Carey, was a silent man who rarely had a pleasant word for anybody. He hated to have young folks around, and it was a mystery to the Rovers why he should occupy a position on a pleasure craft.

"He ought to be on a freight steamer," was Dick's comment—"some boat where he wouldn't meet anybody but those working under him. I can't understand how the captain can bear him for his first assistant."

"The owner of the steam yacht hired him," answered Mr. Rover. "I believe the captain does not like him any more than we do. But the mate does his duty faithfully, so the captain cannot find fault."

Another individual the boys did not like was Bill Bossermann, the assistant engineer. Bossermann was a burly German, with the blackest of hair and a heavy black beard and beady black eyes. He had a coarse voice and manners that put one in mind of a bull. Hans tried to get friendly with him, but soon gave it up.

"He vos von of dem fellers vot knows it all," explained Hans to his chums. "He makes some of dem, vot you call him—bolitical talks, yah. He dinks eferypotty should be so goot like eferypotty else, und chust so rich, too."

"Must be an Anarchist," said Tom. "He looks the part."

"Norton told me he was a first-class engineer," said Dick, "but when I asked him if he was a good fellow he merely shrugged his shoulders in answer."

One day the first mate was in command, the captain having gone below to study his charts and work out the ship's position. Tom had brought a baseball to the deck and was having a catch with Sam. The boys enjoyed the fun for quite a while and did not notice the mate near them.

"Can you throw it up over that rope?" asked Sam, pointing to a stay over his head.

"Sure thing!" cried Tom.

"Look out you don't throw it overboard."

"I'll take care," answered the fun-loving Rover, and launched the baseball high into the air. Just then the steam yacht gave a lurch, the ball hit the mainmast, and down it bounced squarely upon Asa Carey's head, knocking the mate's cap over his eyes and sending him staggering backwards.

"Hi, hi! you young rascals!" roared the mate. "What do you mean by such conduct?"

"Excuse me," replied Tom, humbly. "I didn't mean to hit you. It was an accident."

"I think you did it on purpose, you young villain!"

"It was an accident, Mr. Carey—and I'll thank you not to call me a rascal and a villain," went on Tom rather warmly.

"I'll call you what I please!"

"No, you won't."

"Yes, I will. I am in command here, and I won't have you throwing baseballs at me."

"I just told you it was an accident. If the yacht hadn't rolled just as I threw the ball it would not have hit you."

"Bah! I know boys, and you especially. You love to play tricks on everybody. But you can't play tricks on me." And as the mate spoke he stopped, picked up the rolling ball, and put it in his pocket.

"Are you going to keep that ball?" demanded Sam.

"I am."

"It is our ball."

"See here, Mr. Carey, we didn't mean to hit you, and we were only amusing ourselves catching," said Tom. "We have hired this yacht and we have a right to do as we please on board so long as we don't interfere with the running of the vessel. I want you to give us our ball back." And Tom stepped up and looked the mate squarely in the eyes.

"What! you dare to dictate to me!" roared the mate, and raised his hand as if to strike Tom. He thought the youth would retreat in fear, but Tom never budged.

"I am not trying to dictate, but I have rights as well as you. I want that ball."

"You can't have it."

"If you don't give it to me I shall report the matter to Captain Barforth."

At this threat the mate glared at Tom as if he wanted to eat the boy up.

"If I give you the ball you'll be throwing it at me again," he growled.

"I didn't throw it at you. But as for catching on the deck—I shall ask the captain if that is not allowable. I am quite sure it is, so long as we do no damage."

"Going to sneak behind the captain for protection, eh?" sneered Asa Carey. He did not like the outlook, for that very morning he had had some words with the commander of the steam yacht and had gotten the worst of it.

"I want that ball."

The mate glared at Tom for a moment and then threw the ball to him.

"All right, take your old ball," he muttered. "But you be mighty careful how you use it after this or you'll get into trouble," and with this the mate walked away.

"Are you going to speak to the captain?" asked Sam, in a low tone.

Tom thought for a moment.

"Perhaps it will be better to let it go, Sam. I don't want to stir up any more rows than are necessary. But after this I am going to keep my eye on that fellow."

But if the lads did not mention it to the captain they told their brother and their chums of it, and a long discussion followed.

"I noticed that the mate and the assistant engineer are quite thick," observed Fred. "It seems they were friends before they came aboard."

"And they are two of a kind," remarked Dick. "I feel free to say I do not like than at all."

It was growing warmer, and for the next few days the girls and the boys were content to take it easy under the awnings which had been spread over a portion of the deck. Once the lads amused themselves by fishing with a net and bait, but were not very successful. In the evening they usually sang or played games, and often Songbird would favor them with some of his poetry. For the most of the time Mrs. Stanhope and Mrs. Laning did fancywork.

"Captain says there is a storm coming up," announced Sam, one evening.

"Oh, dear! I hope it doesn't get very rough!" cried Mrs. Stanhope. "I detest a heavy storm at sea."

"Well, mamma, we'll have to expect some storms," said Dora.

"Oh, I shan't mind, if it doesn't thunder and lightning and blow too much."

But this storm was not of the thunder and lightning variety, nor did it blow to any extent. It grew damp and foggy, and then a mist came down over the ocean, shutting out the view upon every side. At once the engine of the steam yacht was slowed down, and a double lookout was stationed at the bow, while the whistle was blown at regular intervals.

"This isn't so pleasant," remarked Songbird, as he and Dick tramped along the deck in their raincoats. "Ugh! what a nasty night it is!"

"No poetry about this, is there, Songbird?" returned Dick, grimly.

"Hardly," said the poet, yet a few minutes later he began softly:

"A dreadful fog came out of the sea,
And made it as misty as it could be.
The deck was wet, the air was damp—"

"It was bad enough to give you a cramp!" finished up Tom, who had come up. "Beautiful weather for drying clothes or taking pictures," he went on. "By the way, I haven't used my new camera yet. I must get it out as soon as the sun shines again."

"And I must get out my camera," said Songbird. "I have a five by seven and I hope to take some very nice pictures when we get down among the islands."

"How do ye like this sea fog?" asked a voice at the boys' rear, and Bahama Bill appeared, wrapped in an oilskin jacket. "It puts me in mind of a fog I onct struck off the coast o' Lower Californy. We was in it fer four days an' it was so thick ye could cut it with a cheese knife. Why, sir, one day it got so thick the sailors went to the bow an' caught it in their hands, jess like that!" He made a grab at the air. "The captain had his little daughter aboard an' the gal went out on deck an' got lost an' we had to feel around in that fog nearly an hour afore we found her, an' then, sure as I'm a standin' here, she was next to drowned an' had to be treated jess like she had been under water."

"How long ago was that?" asked Tom, poking the other boys in the ribs.

"Seven years ago, this very summer."

"I thought so, Bill, for that very summer I was at Fort Nosuch, in Lower California. I remember that fog well. One of the walls of the fort had fallen down and the commander was afraid the desperadoes were going to attack him. So he had the soldiers go out, gather in the fog, and build another wall with it. It made a fine defence, in fact, it was simply out of sight," concluded the fun-loving Rover.

"Say, you—" began Bahama Bill. "You—er—you—say, I can't say another word, I can't! The idee o' building a wall o' fog! Why, say—"

What the old tar wanted to say, or wanted them to say, will never be known, for at that instant came a loud cry from the bow. Almost immediately came a crash, and the *Rainbow* quivered and backed. Then came another crash, and the old sailor and the boys were hurled flat on the deck.

CHAPTER XVII.
A MISHAP IN THE FOG

"We have struck another vessel!"

"We are sinking!"

"How far are we from land?"

These and other cries rang out through the heavy fog, as the two crashes came, followed, a few seconds later, by a third.

Captain Barforth had left the steam yacht in charge of the first mate and was on the companionway going below. With two bounds he was on deck and running toward the bow at top speed.

"What was it? Have we a hole in the bow?" he questioned, of the frightened lookouts, who had been sent spinning across the slippery deck.

"Couldn't make out, captain—it was something black," said one lookout. "Black and square like."

"I think it was a bit of old wreckage," said the other. "Anyway, it wasn't another vessel, and it was too dark for a lumber raft."

"Is it out of sight?"

It was, and though all strained their eyes they could not make out what had been struck, nor did they ever find out.

From the deck the captain made his way below, followed by Mr. Rover, who was anxious to learn the extent of the injuries. In the meantime the ladies and girls had joined the boys on the deck, and the latter began to get out the life preservers.

The most excited man on board was Asa Carey, and without waiting for orders from the captain, he ordered two of the small boats gotten ready to swing overboard. Then he ran down to his stateroom, to get some of his possessions.

"Is we gwine to de bottom?" questioned Aleck, as he appeared, clad in a pair of slippers and a blanket.

"I don't know," answered Fred. "I hope not."

The boys had all they could do to keep the girls quiet, and Grace was on the point of becoming hysterical, which was not to be wondered at, considering the tremendous excitement.

"We cannot be so very far from one of the islands," said Dick. "And if the worst comes to the worst we ought to be able to make shore in the small boats."

"Are there enough boats?" asked Mrs. Laning.

"Yes, the steam yacht is well equipped with them."

The engine of the vessel had been stopped and the steam yacht lay like a log on the rolling waves. The shocks had caused some of the lights to go out, leaving the passengers in semi darkness.

"Oh, Dick, do you think we'll go down?" whispered Dora, as, she clung to his arm.

"Let us hope not, Dora," he answered and caught her closer. "I'll stick to you, no matter what comes!"

"Yes! yes! I want you to do that! And stick to mamma, too!"

"I will. But I don't think we'll go down just yet," he went on, after a long pause. "We seem to be standing still, that's all."

They waited, and as they did so he held her trembling hands tightly in his own. In that minute of extreme peril they realized how very much they were to one another.

At last, after what seemed to be hours, but, was in reality less than five minutes, Anderson Rover appeared.

"There is no immediate danger," said he. "We must have struck some sort of wreckage, or lumber float. There is a small hole in the bow, just above the water line, and several of the seams have been opened. Captain Barforth is having the hole closed up and has started up the donkey pump to keep the water low in the hold. He says he thinks we can make one of the nearby ports without great trouble."

This news removed the tension under which all were suffering, and a little later the ladies and the girls retired to the cabin, and Aleck stole back to his sleeping quarters. The boys went forward, to inspect the damage done, but in the darkness could see little.

"It was an accident such as might happen to any vessel," said the captain, later. "The lookouts were evidently not to blame. There are many derelicts and bits of lumber rafts scattered throughout these waters and consequently traveling at night or in a fog is always more or less dangerous.

"We shall have to put up somewhere for repairs, not so?" questioned Anderson Rover.

"It would be best, Mr. Rover. Of course we might be able to patch things ourselves, but, unless you are in a great hurry, I advise going into port and having it done. It will have to be done sooner or later anyway."

"Where do you advise putting in?"

Captain Barforth thought for a moment.

"I think we had better run over to Nassau, which is less than sixty miles from here. Nassau, as perhaps you know, is the capital city of the Bahamas, and has quite some shipping and we'll stand a good chance there of getting the right ship's—carpenters to do the work."

After some talk, it was decided to steer for Nassau, and the course of the *Rainbow* was changed accordingly. They now ran with even greater caution than before, and a strong searchlight was turned on at the bow, the surplus power from the engine being used for that purpose.

As my young readers may know, Nassau is located on New Providence Island, about two hundred miles east of the lower coast of Florida. It is under British rule and contains about fifteen thousand inhabitants. It is more or less of a health resort and is visited by many tourists, consequently there are several good hotels and many means of spending a few days there profitably.

The run to Nassau was made without further mishaps, and immediately on arriving the steam yacht was placed in the hands of some builders who promised to make the needed repairs without delay. The entire crew remained on board, as did Aleck Pop, but the Rovers and their friends put up at a leading hotel for the time being.

After the run on shipboard from Philadelphia to the Bahamas, the ladies and girls were glad enough to set foot again on land. After one day of quietness at the hotel the party, went out carriage riding, and, of course, the boys went along. They saw not a few unusual sights, and were glad they had their cameras with them.

"We'll have a dandy lot of pictures by the time we get home," said Sam.

"There is one picture I want more than any other," said Tom.

"One of Nellie, I suppose," and Sam winked.

"Oh, I've got that already," answered the fun-loving Rover unabashed.

"What's that you want?" asked Songbird.

"A picture of that treasure cave with us loading the treasure on the yacht."

"Now you are talking, Tom!" cried his older brother. "We all want that. I am sorry we have been delayed here."

"How long vos ve going to sthay here?" questioned Hans.

"The repairs will take the best part of a week, so the ship builders said."

"Ain't you afraid dot Sid Merrick got ahead of you?"

"I don't know. He may be on his way now, or he may not have started yet from New York."

"Oh, I hope we don't meet Merrick, or Sobber either!" cried Dora.

On the outskirts of the town was a fine flower garden where roses of unusual beauty were grown. One day the girls and ladies visited this and Dick and Songbird went along. In the meantime Tom and Sam walked down to the docks, to see how the repairs to the *Rainbow* were progressing, and also to look at the vessels going out and coming in.

"A vessel is due from New York," said Tom. "I heard them talking about it at the hotel."

"Let us see if there is anybody on board we know," answered his brother.

They walked to the spot where the people were to come in, and there learned that the steamer had sent its passengers ashore an hour before. A few were at the dock, taking care of some baggage which had been detained by the custom house officials.

"Well, I never!" exclaimed Tom. "If there isn't Peter Slade! What can he be doing here?"

Peter Slade had once been a pupil at Putnam Hall. He had been something of a bully, although not as bad as Tad Sobber. The boys had often played tricks on him and once Peter had gotten so angry he had left the school and never come back.

"Let us go and speak to him," said Sam.

"Maybe he won't speak, Sam. He was awful angry at us when he left the Hall."

"If he doesn't want to speak he can do the other thing," said the youngest Rover. "Perhaps he'll be glad to meet somebody in this out of the way place."

They walked over to where Peter Slade stood and both spoke at once. The other lad was startled at first and then he scowled.

"Humph! you down here?" he said, shortly.

"Yes," answered Tom, pleasantly enough. "Did you just get in on the steamer?"

"I don't know as that is any of your business, Tom Rover!"

"It isn't, and if you don't want to speak civilly, Slade, you haven't got to speak at all," said Tom, and started to move away, followed by his brother.

"Say, did you meet Tad Sobber and his un—" And then Peter Slade stopped short in some confusion.

"Did we meet who?" demanded Tom, wheeling around in some astonishment.

"Never mind," growled Peter Slade.

"Were they on the steamer?" asked Sam.

"I'm not saying anything about it."

"Look here, Slade, if they were on the steamer we want to know it," came from Tom.

"Really?" and the former bully of the Hall put as much of a sneer as possible into the word.

"We do, and you have got to tell us."

"I don't see why."

"You will if you are honest," said Sam. "You know as well as I do that Tad Sobber's uncle is a rascal and ought to be in prison."

"Tad says it isn't so—that his uncle didn't take those bonds— that they were placed in his care to be sold at a profit, if possible."

"When did Tad tell you that?"

"Only a couple of days ago—I mean he told me, and that's enough."

"Then he told you while you were on the steamer," put in Tom.

"Yes, if you must know." Peter Slade's face took on a cunning look. "I guess Mr. Merrick and Tad will trim you good and proper soon."

"What do you mean by that?"

"Oh, I know a thing or two."

"Did they tell you what had brought them down here?"

"Maybe they did."

"Who was with them?"

"You had better ask them."

"Where are they?"

"That's for you to find out."

"See here, Slade, this is no way to talk," went on Tom earnestly. "If you know anything about Sid Merrick and his plans you had better tell us about them. If you don't I shall take it for granted that you are in league with that rascal and act accordingly."

"Yes, and that may mean arrest for you," added Sam.

Peter Slade was a coward at heart, and these suggestive words made him turn pale.

"I am not in league with them," he cried hastily. "I met them on the steamer by accident. Tad told me he and his uncle were going to get the best of you, but how he didn't say."

"Who was with them, come, out with it."

"A Spaniard named Doranez."

"Doranez!" cried both the Rover boys and looked suggestively at each other.

"Yes, do you know him?"

"We know of him," answered Tom slowly. "Where did they go?"

"I don't know exactly."

"Don't you know at all?"

"They were going to look for some tramp steamer that was to be here. If they found her they were going to sail at once to some other island," answered Peter Slade.

CHAPTER XVIII.
THE NEW DECK HAND

Having said so much, Peter Slade seemed more inclined to talk, one reason being that he wanted to get at the bottom of the mystery which had brought Tad Sobber and his uncle to that part of the globe. Tad had hinted of great wealth, and of getting the best of the Rovers and some other people, but had not gone into any details.

Peter said he had come to Nassau to join his mother, who was stopping there for her health. His father was coming on later, and then the family was going across the ocean.

"I know there is something up between your crowd and the Merrick crowd," said the youth. "You are both after something, ain't you?"

"Yes," answered Tom.

"What?"

"I can't tell you that, Slade. It's something quite valuable, though."

"Well, I guess Sobber's uncle will get ahead of you."

"Perhaps so. What is the name of the tramp steamer he is looking for?"

"The *Josephine*."

"Was she to be here?"

"They hoped she would be."

"Were they going to hire her?" asked Sam.

"I suppose so."

"Then Merrick had money."

"Yes, he had some, and that Spaniard had some, too."

A little more conversation followed, and then the Rover boys asked Slade where he was going to stop, and said they might see him later.

"This is mighty interesting," remarked Tom, as he and his brother hurried to their hotel. "We must tell father of this without delay."

But Mr. Rover could not be found until that evening, when the party came back from the visit to the flower gardens. He listened with deep interest to what was said, and then went off on a hunt for Sid Merrick and the tramp steamer *Josephine* without delay.

Nothing was discovered that night, but a little before noon of the day following they learned that a tramp steamer had appeared in the harbor, taken several persons on board, and then steamed away again.

"Can you tell me the name of that craft?" asked Anderson Rover of the man who gave him this information.

"She was the *Josephine*, sir, of Charleston, Captain Sackwell."

"Was she loaded?"

"I think not, sir."

"How many persons got aboard?"

"Five or six."

"One of them a young fellow?"

"Yes, sir, and one was a fellow who was very dark."

Mr. Rover knew that Doranez was very dark, and he rightfully surmised that the party had been made up of Merrick, Tad, Doranez, Cuffer and Shelley.

"This is certainly a serious turn of affairs," said he to his sons. "While we have been losing time in Philadelphia and elsewhere, Sid Merrick has gone to work, gotten somebody to let him have this tramp steamer, and now, in company with Doranez, is off to locate Treasure Isle and the treasure. It looks to me as if it might be a race between us after all."

"Yes, and the worst of it is that we are laid up for repairs," said Dick, with almost a groan in his voice.

"How long must we remain here?" asked Sam "Can't they hurry the job somehow?"

"Let us offer 'em more money to hurry," suggested Tom.

The suggestion to offer more money was carried out, and the ship builders promised to have the *Rainbow* fit for sailing by the following afternoon. The paint on the new work would not be dry, but that would not matter.

On the morning of the day they were to sail a man applied to Captain Barforth for a position. He said he had been a fireman on an ocean liner, but had lost three fingers in some machinery and been discharged.

"I am hard up," he pleaded. "I'll work for almost anything."

The captain was kind hearted, and as the *Rainbow* could use another deck hand he told the man to bring his luggage aboard, which the fellow did. The newcomer's name was Walt Wingate, and he did his best to make friends with everybody on board. He had a low, musical voice, and was frequently whistling popular airs.

"He's an odd one," said Dick, after noticing the new deck hand several times. "He seems real nice and yet—"

"You don't like him," finished Sam.

"That's it, Sam."

"Neither do I, and I can't tell why."

"Well, he hasn't anything to do with us. If he's a good man I'm glad the captain gave him a job. It's tough luck to lose your fingers, especially if you must work for a living."

By five o'clock the steam yacht had left the harbor of Nassau and was standing out to sea once more. The course was again southward, around the western extremity of Cuba. During the following days they passed numerous islands and keys, as they are called, but generally at such a distance that the shores could be seen but faintly.

To make sure of what he was doing, Anderson Rover held several consultations with Captain Barforth, and Bahama Bill was closely questioned regarding the location of Treasure Isle. The old tar stuck to the story he had told so often, and went over numerous maps with the commander of the steam yacht.

"He has the location pretty well fixed in his head unless the whole thing is a fairy tale," was Captain Barforth's comment.

While one of these talks was going on, Dick, who was on deck, chanced to go below in a hurry. As he passed down the companionway he encountered Walt Wingate, who had been listening at the cabin doorway.

"Hullo, what do you want?" demanded Dick, for the man's face had a guilty look on it.

"Why—er—my handkerchief blew down here and I came down to get it," answered the new deck hand, and pointed to the cloth in question sticking out of his pocket.

"Is that all?"

"That's all, sir," answered Wingate, and touching his cap he slouched off. Then he turned back. "Sorry if I disturbed anybody," he added.

"Oh, I suppose it is all right," returned Dick, but he was by no means satisfied, although he could not tell exactly why. There was something about the new deck hand that did not "ring true." At first he thought to speak to his parent about the occurrence, but then concluded not to worry his father.

Knowing that it was now a race between the *Rainbow* and the *Josephine* for Treasure Isle, Captain Barforth crowded on all steam. The course of the steam yacht was fairly well laid out, but it contained many turns and twists, due to the many keys—located in these waters.

"We don't want to run on any hidden reef," said the master of the vessel. "If we do we may go down or be laid up for a long while for repairs. These waters are fairly well charted, but there is still a great deal to be learned about them. From time to time they have had earthquakes down here, and volcano eruptions, and the bottom is constantly shifting."

On the second night out from Nassau, Sam, for some reason, could not sleep. He tumbled and tossed in his berth for two hours, and then, feeling that some fresh air might do him good, dressed in part and went on deck.

It was not a very clear night, and but few stars shone in the firmament. In the darkness the lad walked first to one side of the steam yacht and then to the other. Then he strolled toward the bow, to have a little chat with the lookout.

As he walked along the side of the cabin he became aware of a figure leaning over the rail, gazing far down into the sea. By the man's general form he made the fellow out to be Walt Wingate. The deck hand had hold of something, although what it was Sam could not tell.

At first the youngest Rover was going to call to the man and ask him what he was doing. But he remained silent, and stepped into the shadow of the cabin as Wingate left the rail and crossed to the other side of the yacht. From under some coils of rope the deck hand brought forth something, lifted it over the rail and dropped it gently into the sea. Then he leaned far over the rail as before, and this lasted two or three minutes.

"He is certainly up to something out of the ordinary," thought Sam. "I wonder if he is fishing? If he is, it seems to me it is a queer way to go at it."

As Wingate left the rail he walked directly to where the boy stood. When he discovered Sam he started back as if confronted by a ghost.

"Oh—er—didn't know anybody was up," he stammered.

"It was so hot in my stateroom I couldn't sleep," answered Sam. "I came out to get the air."

"It's almost as hot on deck as it is anywhere," said the deck hand, and his tone had little of cordiality in it.

"I think I'll go forward and try it there."

"Yes, it's a little breezier at the bow, sir. By the way, did you—er—see me trying to catch some of those firefish just now?"

"I saw you doing something, I didn't see what."

"I thought I might get one, but they are all gone now," answered Wingate, and slouched off, whistling in that peculiar manner of his.

Sam walked slowly to the bow. As he did this, Wingate turned to look at him in a speculative way.

"Wonder if the young fool saw what I was up to?" he muttered. "If he did I'd better go slow. I don't want to get caught. They might treat me pretty roughly."

The watch on deck was changed and Wingate went below. Asa Carey was in command of the yacht and he, too, wanted to know why Sam was up at such a late hour. The boy told him, but said nothing to the mate of Wingate's strange actions.

When Sam turned in, Dick wanted to know if he was sick.

"No, only restless, Dick," he replied. "By the way, I saw something strange," he continued, and he related the occurrence.

"We must look into this, Sam. It may mean nothing and it may mean a great deal," was the eldest Rover boy's comment.

The boys did not go on deck until after breakfast. Then they walked to the starboard rail and stopped at the spot where Sam had first discovered the deck hand.

"I don't see anything," said Dick, gazing over the rail. "Perhaps he was fishing, after all. He may have thought—Hullo!"

"What is it, Dick?"

"Some kind of a line down here—a wire, fastened to a hook!"

"Can you reach it?"

"Hardly. I might if you'll hold my legs, so I don't go overboard."

"Hadn't we better tell Captain Barforth of this first? The wire may belong there."

"I don't know what for. But we can tell the captain. Here he comes now."

"Good morning, boys," said the master of the steam yacht pleasantly. "What can you see over there?"

"Something we think unusual," said Sam "Please take a look and tell us what it is."

Captain Barforth did as requested.

"That wire has no business there," he declared. "I don't know how it came there."

"I can tell you how it got there, and I guess you'll find something like it on the other side," answered Sam, and told what he had seen Wingate do during the night.

"Humph, I'll investigate this," muttered the captain, and went off for a boathook. When he returned he caught the hook into the loop of the wire and tried to bring the end of the strand to the deck. He was unable to do it alone and had to get the boys to aid him. Then all three ran the wire around a brace and gradually hauled it aboard. At the end was an iron chain, fastened into several loops, and also the anchor to one of the rowboats.

CHAPTER XIX.
TREASURE ISLE AT LAST

"So this is the work of that new deck hand, eh?" cried Captain Barforth, grimly. "A fine piece of business to be in, I must say!"

"Let us see what is on the other side?" suggested Dick.

This was done, and they brought up another wire, to the end of which were attached two small anchors and some pieces of scrap steel from the tool room.

"He put those overboard for drag anchors," explained the master of the steam yacht. "He did it to delay the *Rainbow*."

"Yes, and that was done so the *Josephine* could get ahead of us," added Dick.

"In that case he must be in league with Sid Merrick," came from Sam.

"Perhaps he met Merrick at Nassau and was hired for this work," said Dick.

"That is possible, Dick. I'll have the truth out of him, if I have to put him in irons and on bread and water to do it," added Captain Barforth.

He at once sent for Walt Wingate. The deck hand who went after the man came back five minutes later to report that the fellow could not be located.

"He must be found!" cried Captain Barforth. "He can't skulk out of this!"

A search was instituted, in which all of the boys, Mr. Rover and Aleck joined. But though the steam yacht was searched from stem to stern, the missing deck hand was not located. Some of the men even went down into the hold, but with no success.

"Do you think he jumped overboard?" asked Fred.

"He might, but it would be a foolish thing to do," answered the captain. "We are at least ten miles from any island."

"He may have had a small boat," said Songbird.

"No, the small boats are all here. He is on this vessel, but where is the question."

To stimulate them in their search, the captain offered a reward of ten dollars to any one of his crew who should bring Wingate to light. But this brought no success, and for a very good reason as we shall learn later.

How much the drags had hampered the progress of the *Rainbow* there was no telling, but freed of them, the steam yacht made good time. All of the machinery was carefully inspected, including the propeller, to which some wire was found twisted. But this had thus far done no damage and was easily pulled out.

"He is certainly in league with Merrick and his crowd," said Anderson Rover, "and that being so, we must be on constant guard against him."

The ladies and the girls were much alarmed to think that such a character as Wingate might be roaming around the vessel in secret, and at night they locked every stateroom door with care. The boys and Mr. Rover were also on the alert, and some of them slept with loaded pistols near at hand. Had Wingate shown himself unexpectedly he might have met with a warm reception.

"That feller's disappearance puts me in mind o' something that happened aboard the *Nancy Belden*, bound from the Congo to New York, jest eight years ago this summer," said Bahama Bill, who had searched as hard as anybody for the missing man. "We had on board a lot o' wild animals fer a circus man, an' amongst 'em, was an orang outang, big an' fierce, I can tell you. Well, this orang outang got out o' his cage one night, an' in the mornin' he couldn't be found. We hunted an' hunted, an' the next night nobody wanted to go to sleep fer fear he'd wake up dead. The cap'n had his family aboard and the wife she was 'most scart stiff an' wouldn't hardly leave her room."

"And did you find the orang outang?" asked Songbird, with interest.

"We did an' we didn't. The fifth night after he was missing we heard a fearful noise right in a cage wot had a lion in it. We run to the place with shootin' irons an' spears and capstan bars, thinkin' the lion was loose. When we got there we found the orang outang had twisted one o' the bars o' the cage loose an' got inside and disturbed Mr. Lion's best nap. Mr. Lion didn't like it, an' he gets up, and in about two minutes he makes mince meat o' the orang outang. When we got there all we see was bits o' skin, an' the feet an' head o' the orang outang, yes, sir. We was glad he was gone—especially the cap'n wife—but the circus men was mad to lose sech a valerable beast," concluded Bahama Bill.

"That was a pretty good one," was Tom's comment. "Too good to be spoiled," and at this remark the others laughed.

"Vell, it's someding like ven dot snake got loose py Putnam Hall," was Hans' comment. "Dot Vingate vos noddings put a snake, hey?"

"You hit it that time, Hans," answered Dirk, "A snake and of the worst kind."

According to Bahama Bill's reckoning they were now less than two days' sailing from Treasure Isle, and all on board who were in the secret were filled with expectancy. So far nothing had been seen of the *Josephine*, and they Wondered if the tramp steamer was ahead of them, or if they had passed her in the darkness.

"Of course, she may have come by a different route," said Captain Barforth. "While we passed to the east and south of some of the little islands she may have gone to the north and west of them. One route would be about as good as the other."

That night it grew foggy, and as a consequence they had to slow down, which filled the boys with vexation for, as Tom declared, "they wanted to find that island and the treasure right away."

"Well, you'll have to be patient," said Nellie,

"Aren't you anxious, Nellie?" he asked.

"Oh, yes, Tom; but I don't want to see anybody hurt, or the yacht sunk."

Twenty four hours later the fog rolled away and on the following morning Captain Barforth announced they were in the locality where Treasure Isle was supposed to be located. The boys stationed themselves in various parts of the steam yacht, and Dick and Tom went aloft with a good pair of marine glasses.

"I see an island!" cried Tom, half an hour later.

This announcement thrilled all on board, but an hour later it was discovered that the island was only a small affair and Bahama Bill promptly said it was not that for which they were seeking.

"Come aloft and look through the glass," said Dick to the old tar, and Bahama Bill readily accepted the invitation. Thus two hours more went by, and the course of the steam yacht was changed to a wide circle.

"More land!" cried Dick, presently. "What do you make of that?" he asked and handed the marine glasses to Bahama Bill.

The old tar looked through the glasses for a long time and then put them down with much satisfaction.

"That's the place, or I'll forfeit a month's wages," he said.

"Is it Treasure Isle?" burst out Tom.

"Yes."

"Hurrah!" shouted Tom, running down the ratlines to the deck. "We've found the island!" he shouted. "Hurrah!"

"Where?" asked half a dozen at once.

"Over in that direction. You can't see it with the naked eye, but it's there just the same. Hurrah!" And in his high spirits Tom did a few steps of a fancy jig.

Without delay the bow of the steam yacht was pointed in the direction of the land that had been discovered, and after awhile all made it out, a mere speck on the blue water. But as they approached, the speck grew larger and larger, and they saw it was a beautiful tropical isle, with waving palms reaching down almost to the water's edge.

"We can't land on this side," announced Bahama Bill. "The sea is too dangerous here, We'll have to sail around to the south shore and lay to beyond the reef, and then take small boats to the inside of the horseshoe."

Again the course of the *Rainbow* was changed, and they skirted the eastern shore of the island, which was truly shaped like a horseshoe, with the opening on the south side. To the north, the east and the west were smaller islands and reefs, sticking out, "like horseshoe nails," as Sam said. Sailing was dangerous here, and they had to go slow and make frequent soundings, so that they did not reach the south side of Treasure Isle until almost nightfall.

"The same old place!" murmured Bahama Bill.

"An' we anchored right out here when we took that treasure ashore! I remember it as well if it was yesterday!" And he nodded over and over again.

"And where is the cave from here?" asked Mr. Rover, who was as anxious as anybody to locate the treasure.

"You can't see it, because it's behind the trees an' rocks," replied the tar.

The reef beyond the horseshoe was a dangerous one, with the sea dashing up many feet over it. There was only one break, less than thirty feet wide, so gaining entrance to the harbor would be no easy matter in a rowboat. "We had better wait until morning before we go ashore," said Captain Barforth. "Even if we land we'll be able to do little in the darkness."

"Oh, don't wait!" pleaded Tom.

"Why can't some of us go ashore?" put in Sam, who was as impatient as his brother.

"I'd like to go myself," added Dick, "even if I had to stay ashore all night. Remember, the *Josephine* is on the way here, and the sooner some of us get to land and locate that cave the better."

"The *Josephine* isn't here yet," said Fred.

"No, but she may put in an appear at any time," answered Tom. "I believe in taking time by the forelock, as the saying is."

The matter was talked over for a few minutes, and then it was decided to let Tom, Dick, and Sam go ashore in company with two sailors, who would then bring the rowboat back to the steam yacht. The boys were to take blankets and some provisions with them and spend the night on the island.

"I don't think you'll find the cave without Bahama Bill's aid," said Mr. Rover. "But it will do no harm to look around. If this isle is like the rest of the West Indies there will be little on it to hurt you. There are few wild animals down here, and no savages outside of some negroes who occasionally go on a spree and cut loose.."

The rowboat was soon ready, and the boys embarked, with the best wishes of those left behind. Hans wanted to go very much, but was told he must wait until morning. Bahama Bill said he would rather sleep on shipboard any time than on shore.

"A bunk for me," were his words. "It's better than under the trees or bushes. Once I was ashore sleepin' an' a big snake crawled over my legs. I thought some cannibals were trying to tie me fast and jumped up. When I see the snake I run about three miles without stopping. A bunk fer me every time, yes, sir!"

It was exciting to bring the rowboat through the passage of the reef and once the boys thought they were going to ship a good deal of water. But the two men who were rowing knew their business and brought them into the horseshoe harbor without mishap. They helped the lads to land, on a small sandy strip close to some palms, and then started back to the steam yacht.

"Treasure Isle at last!" cried Dick, when they were left alone. "So far our quest has been successful. Now to locate the cave and unearth that treasure!"

"And may it prove to be worth all that has been said of it," added Sam

CHAPTER XX.
THE BOYS MAKE A DISCOVERY

The boys had landed at a spot that was particularly inviting in appearance, and they stopped for several minutes to take in the natural beauty surrounding them. There were tall and stately palms, backed up by other trees, trailing vines of great length, and numerous gorgeous flowers. A sweet scent filled the air, and from the woods in the center of the isle came the song of tropical birds.

"What a fine camping place!" murmured Sam. "A fellow could spend several weeks here and have lots of fun, bathing and boating, and hunting birds, and fishing," and his brothers agreed with him.

Yet the beauty of Treasure Isle was soon forgotten in their anxiety to locate the cave. They had a general idea that it was in the center of the horseshoe curve, and that center was quite a distance from where they had been brought ashore.

"The best we can do is to tramp along the water's edge," said Dick. "Then when we reach the center we can go inland."

"We haven't over an hour," replied his youngest brother. "By that time it will be too dark to do much more. And we'll have to find some suitable place to camp for the night."

"Oh, we can camp anywhere," cried Tom. "It's good enough—just for one night."

They began to trudge along the edge of the horseshoe curve, over smooth sand. But this did not last, and presently they came to a muddy flat and went down to their ankles. Dick was ahead and he cried to the others.

"Stop! It's not fit to walk here!"

"Why, it's like a bog!" declared Sam, after testing it.

"We'll have to go inland a distance," said Tom. "Come on," and he turned back and struck out for the palms and bushes beyond.

It was then that the Rover boys began to realize what was before them. Scarcely had they penetrated the interior for fifty yards when they found themselves in a perfect network of trailing vines. Then, after having pulled and cut their way through for fifty yards more, they came to a spot that was rocky and covered with a tangle of thorny bushes.

"Wow!" ejaculated Tom, after scratching his hand and his leg. "This is something prime, I must confess!"

"What I call hunting a treasure with a vengeance," added Dick, dryly.

"I move we go back," came from Sam. "We seem to be stuck in more ways than one."

"Perhaps it is better traveling just beyond," declared Dick. "I am not going to turn back just yet anyway."

He took the lead, breaking down the thorny bushes as best he could, and Sam and Tom followed closely in his footsteps. It was rather dark among the bushes and almost before the three knew it they had fallen headlong into a hollow.

"Well, I never!"

"This is coming down in a hurry!"

"Is this the treasure cave?"

Such were the exclamations of the three lads as they picked themselves up out of the dirt, which, fortunately for them, was soft and yielding. Nobody had been hurt, for which they were thankful.

The hollow was about fifty feet in diameter and half that depth in the center. On the opposite side were more bushes and rocks, and then a thicket of tall trees of a variety that was strange to them.

"This is what I call hard work," observed Tom, as they began to fight their way along again. "I don't know but what we would have done as well to have waited until morning."

"Don't croak, Tom," said Sam.

"Oh, I am not croaking, but this is no fun, let me tell you that."

All of the boys were panting from their exertions, and soon they had to call a halt to get their breath. It was now growing dark rapidly, for in the tropics there is little of what we know as twilight.

"We certainly can't do much more in this darkness," said Dick at last. "I must confess I thought walking in the direction of the cave would be an easy matter."

"Well, what's to do next?" questioned Sam, gazing around in perplexity.

This was no easy question to answer. As if by magic darkness had settled all around them, shutting out the sight of objects less than a hundred yards away. To go forward was all but impossible, and whether or not they could get back to where they had come from was a serious problem.

"If we can't get back we'll have to camp right here," said Dick.

But they did not want to stay in such a thicket and so they pushed on a little further, until they reached a slight rise of ground. Then Dick, who was in advance as before, uttered a cry of surprise:

"A trail! I wonder where it leads to?"

He was right, a well defined trail or footpath lay before them, running between the brushwood and palms and around the rocks. It did not look as if it had been used lately, but it was tolerably clear of any growth.

This was something the Rover boys had not counted on, for Bahama Bill had never spoken of any trail in his descriptions of the isle. They gazed at the path with curiosity. Tom was the first to speak.

"Shall we follow it?" he asked.

"Might as well," answered Sam. "It's better than scratching yourself and tearing your clothing in those thorn bushes."

The boys took to the trail and passed along for a distance of quarter of a mile or more. It wound in and out around the rocks and trees and had evidently been made by some natives bringing out wild fruits and the like from the forest.

"It doesn't seem to be leading us to anywhere," was Dick's comment. "I don't know whether to go on or not."

Nevertheless, they kept on, until they came to a sharp turn around a series of rocks. As they, moved ahead they suddenly saw a glare of light cross the rocks and then disappear.

"What was that?" asked Sam, somewhat startled.

"A light," answered Dick.

"I know. But where did it come from?"

"It was like the flash of a bicycle gas lamp," said Tom.

"There are no bicycles on this trail," said Dick.

"I know that, too, Dick. But it was like that kind of a lamp."

Just then the flash of light reappeared, and now they saw it came from a point on the trail ahead of them. They listened intently and heard somebody approaching.

"Several men are coming!" whispered Dick.

"Not from our yacht?" said Tom.

"I don't think so."

"Can they be from the *Josephine*?" asked Sam.

"That remains to be seen."

"If they are from the *Josephine* what shall we do?"

"I think the best thing we can do is to keep out of sight and watch them."

"But they may locate the cave and take the treasure away," said Tom.

"We have got to run that risk unless we want to fight them."

"Oh, if only we could get our crowd here to help us!" murmured Sam.

"We may be mistaken and they may be strangers to us. Come, let us hide."

Losing no time, the three Rover boys stepped into the bushes beside the trail. As they did so the other party came closer, and the lads saw that they carried not only an acetylene gas lamp, but also a ship's lantern and several other things. The party was made up of Sid Merrick, Tad Sobber, Cuffer and Shelley.

"It's mighty rough walking here," they heard Tad Sobber complain. "I've got a thorn right through my shoe. Wait till I pull it out, will you?" And he came to a halt not over ten yards from where the Rover boys were hidden.

"You didn't have to come, Tad," said his uncle, somewhat harshly. "I told you to suit yourself."

"Oh, I want to see that treasure cave as well as you do," answered Sobber.

"I'd like to know if this is the right trail or not," came from Shelley. "You ought to have brought that Spaniard along, to make sure."

"Doranez is no good!" growled Sid Merrick who was by no means in the best of humor. "He likes his bottle too well. If he would only keep sober it would be different."

"Why don't you take his liquor from him?" asked Cuffer. "I'd do it quick enough if I was running this thing."

"He says he won't tell us a thing more if we cut off his grog. He is getting mighty ugly."

"Maybe he wants to sell out to those Rovers," suggested Shelley.

"He wouldn't dare to do that—I know too much about him," answered Sid Merrick. "No, it's because he wants too big a share of the treasure."

"Do you suppose the fellows on the steam yacht have landed here yet?" asked Tad, as he prepared to go on.

"I don't know. They are laying to outside of the reef. I reckon they don't know anything of the landing on the other side of the island," answered his uncle. "Come on, we haven't any time to waste if we want to head them off. I didn't dream they'd get here so quickly."

"I guess that fellow Wingate was no good," came from Cuffer. "He didn't delay the steam yacht in the least."

"Maybe he got caught at his funny work," suggested Shelley, hitting the nail directly on the head, as the reader already knows.

Casting the light of the acetylene gas lamp ahead of them, the party from the *Josephine* moved on, directly past the spot where the

Rovers were in hiding. The boys hardly dared to breathe for fear of discovery. They stood stock still until the others were all but out of sight.

"This is interesting," murmured Tom. "They must have landed on the other side of the island."

"Yes, and Merrick hired that Walt Wingate to play us foul!" cried Sam. "What shall we do next, Dick?" he continued anxiously. "They act as if they expect to get that treasure to night!"

"I don't know what to do exactly," answered Dick. "But one thing is certain—we must follow them up and prevent their getting hold of that treasure if we possibly can!"

CHAPTER XXI.
SCARING OFF THE ENEMY

It was easy enough for Dick to say they must follow up their enemies and prevent Sid Merrick and his party from gaining possession of the treasure, but how all this was to be accomplished was another matter.

In the first place, the other party numbered four as against their three. More than this, those from the *Josephine* were heavily armed, while the Rovers had brought with them nothing but a single pistol.

"It's well enough to talk," whispered Sam, after Sid Merrick and his crowd had passed on, "but if we tackle them in the open the chances are we'll get the worst of it."

"We may get a chance at them in some other way," answered Dick. "We have this advantage, we know where they are and they don't know we are on the isle."

With cautious steps they stole after the Merrick party, keeping them in sight by the waving rays of the lamp and lantern ahead, as they danced over the rocks and among the trees and bushes. They kept about a hundred feet to the rear.

"I've got a plan," said Tom, as the party ahead came to a halt to make sure of the trail. "Can't we cut in somewhere and get ahead of them and then scare them back?"

"Let's try it!" exclaimed Sam. "I am sure if we play ghosts, or something like that, we'll scare Tad Sobber out of his wits."

"It's a risky thing to do," mused the eldest Rover. "We might get caught at it."

Nevertheless, he was rather in favor of the plan, and when the Merrick party stopped again, for Cuffer to take a stone out of his shoe, they "cut into" the woods and pushed forward with all speed. It was hard work, but they were in deadly earnest, and did not let the vines and brushwood deter them.

"Now, the question is, How are we to scare them?" said Dick, after they had regained the trail, well in advance of Sid Merrick and his followers.

"Let us play ghosts?" said Sam.

"We might black up and play niggers on the warpath, with big clubs," suggested Tom.

"And get shot down," interrupted Dick. "No, I think the ghosts idea is as good as anything. Quick, take off your coats and tie your handkerchiefs over your faces."

The boys had on light colored outing shirts, and these, with the handkerchiefs over their faces, made them look quite ghostlike in the gloom under the trees.

"Now, when the time comes groan," said Tom "Ghosts always groan, you know."

"And let us order them back," added Sam.

"But be sure to do it in very ghostlike tones," warned Dick. "If our voices sound a bit natural they'll get suspicious at once. If they come for us, or shoot at us, drop behind the rocks and run into the woods."

It must be confessed that the boys were doubtful of the success of their ruse. Yet they felt they must do something to hold the treasure seeking party in check, at least until morning. With the coming of daylight they could signal to the *Rainbow* and with the aid of those on the steam yacht probably rout the enemy.

The Rover boys advanced along the trail until they reached a spot they deemed favorable for their purpose. Then Dick gave his brothers a few more directions.

Presently they saw the rays of the gas lamp and the lantern in the distance. At once Tom set up a deep groaning and Sam and Dick joined in.

"What's that?" asked Shelley, who was the first to hear the sounds.

"Sounds like somebody in distress," answered Sid Merrick.

"Thought you said there was nobody on this island?" came from Cuffer.

"Didn't think there was. Maybe it's some native who—"

"Look! look!" screamed Tad Sobber and pointed ahead with his hand. "What's that?"

"What's what?" asked the men in concert.

"There—that thing bobbing up and down over the rocks?" And Tad Sobber trembled as he spoke. This lonely walk through the darkness of the forest had somewhat unnerved him.

"That's strange," muttered Merrick. "It's groaning!"

"It's a ghost!" screamed Tad, and shrank back, as did Cuffer and Shelley.

"A ghost?" repeated Sid Merrick. "Nonsense! There are no such things as ghosts."

"It cer-certainly looks like a-a ghost!" faltered Cuffer.

"It is a ghost!" said Tad, his teeth beginning to chatter. "I-I ca-can hear it gro-groan! Come on ba-ba-back!" And he began to retreat.

"Back with you!" came in solemn tones. "Back with you!"

"No white man must come here," said a second voice. "This is sacred ground!"

"He who sets foot here dies!" came from a third voice. "This is the burial place of the great Hupa hupa! Back, if you value your life!" And then followed a jabbering nobody could understand, and white arms were waved wildly in the air.

This warning was too much for Tad Sobber, and without further ado he took to his heels and retreated down the trail whence he had come. Cuffer followed him, and Shelley also retreated several yards.

"Stop, you fools!" cried Sid Merrick. "Those are no ghosts, I tell you. It's a trick of some kind."

"I—I don't know about that," answered Shelley. "Don't you think it would be better to come here in the daylight? We—er—we can't find that cave in the dark anyway."

"Yes, we can—and I am going to do it, too," was Merrick's answer. "That is a trick, I tell you." He raised his voice: "Who are you?" he called out. "Answer me truthfully, or I'll fire on you!"

This threat alarmed the Rover boys, for they saw that Merrick was in earnest.

"I guess our cake is dough," muttered Tom.

"Wait, I think I can scare him back yet," said Dick. "Let me do the talking."

"I say, who are you?" repeated Merrick. "You needn't pretend to be ghosts, for I don't believe in them."

"We are the owners of this isle," answered Dick, in the heaviest tone he could assume. "We are ten strong, and we order you to go back to your ship at once."

"The owners of this isle?"

"Yes."

"I don't believe it."

"You can do as you please about that. But if you come a yard further we'll fire at you."

"Humph! Then you are armed?"

"We are and we know how to shoot, too."

"What brought you here at such a time as this?"

"We have a special reason for being here, as you may learn by to morrow."

"Do you know anything of a treasure on this island?" went on Sid Merrick curiously.

"We know something of it, yes. It belongs to the Stanhope estate, provided it can be found."

"It doesn't belong to the Stanhopes at all—it belongs to me," cried Merrick.

"In a day or two the Stanhopes are coming here to take possession," went on Dick. "They will bring with them a number of their friends and uncover the treasure, which is now hidden in a secret place. As I and my brothers and cousins own this isle we are to have our share of what is uncovered. Now we warn you again to go away. We are ten to your four, and we are all armed with shotguns and pistols, and we have the drop on you."

"Good for you, Dick, pile it on," whispered Tom. Then he pulled Sam by the arm. "Come on, let us appear from behind another rock—they'll think we are two more of the brothers or cousins!"

"You won't dare to shoot us," blustered Merrick, but his voice had a trace of uncertainty in it.

"Won't we?" answered Dick. "There is a warning for you!" And raising the pistol he carried he sent a shot over the heads of the other party.

"They are shooting at us! We'll all be killed!" yelled Tad Sobber, who had come back during the conversation, and again he and Cuffer took to their heels.

"Mind the warning!" called out Dick, and dropped almost out of sight behind a rock. At that same moment Tom and Sam appeared from behind a rock far to the left.

"Mind that warning!" they cried. "Remember, we are ten to four!"

"There are two more of 'em," cried Shelley.

"Confound the luck, what sort of a game is this anyway?" said Sid Merrick, much chagrined.

"Well, it is more than we expected," answered Shelley. "I, for one, don't care to risk being shot down. I reckon they have the bulge on us, if there really are ten of 'em."

"I've seen but five the three ahead and the two over yonder."

"There are two more!" answered Shelley and pointed to another rock, to which Sam and Tom had just crawled. "That makes seven."

"Go back, I tell you," warned Dick. "We'll give you just two minutes in which to make up your mind. If you don't go back we'll start to shoot!"

"Come on back!" cried Tad, from a safe distance. "Don't let them shoot you, Uncle Sid!"

"We'll go back to our ship," called out Sid Merrick. "But remember, this thing isn't settled yet."

"If you have any differences with the Stanbopes you can settle with the folks on the steam yacht which has just arrived," answered Dick, not knowing what else to say.

The party under Sid Merrick began to retreat, and Dick, Tom and Sam watched them with interest, until the lights faded in the distance. Then Tom did a jig in his delight.

"That was easier than I expected," he said.

"Even if we didn't scare them playing ghost," added Sam. "I wonder if they really thought we were ten in number?"

"Well, they thought we were seven anyway!" answered Dick. "It was a clever ruse you two played."

What to do next the Rover boys did not know. It was impossible for any of them to calculate how far they were from the spot where they had landed or to determine the best way of getting back to Foreshow Bay, as they had named the locality.

"If we move around very much in this darkness we may become hopelessly lost in the forest," said Dick.

"Maybe we had better stay right where we are until morning," suggested his youngest brother.

"I'm agreeable to anything," were Tom's words.

"If we stay here we want to remain on guard," said Dick. "Merrick may take it into his head to come back."

An hour later found the three Rover boys encamped in a small opening to one side of the forest trail. They made beds for themselves of some soft brushwood, and it was decided that one should remain on guard while the other two slept.

"Each can take three hours of guard duty," said Dick. "That will see us through the night nicely," and so it was arranged.

CHAPTER XXII.
PRISONERS IN THE FOREST

Dick was the first to go on guard and during the initial hour of his vigil practically nothing came to disturb him. He heard the occasional cry of the nightbirds and the booming of the surf on the reefs and the shore of the isle, and saw numerous fireflies flit to and fro, and that was all.

"I don't believe they'll come back," he murmured to himself. "Like as not they are afraid to advance on the trail and also afraid to trust themselves to this jungle in the darkness."

Dick had found some wild fruit growing close at hand and he began to sample this. But it was bitter, and he feared to eat much, thinking it might make him sick. Then, to keep awake, for he felt sleepy because of his long tramp, he took out his knife and began to cut his initials on a stately palm growing beside the temporary camp.

Dick had just finished one letter and was starting the next when of a sudden he found himself caught from behind. His arms were pinned to his side, his pistol wrenched from his grasp, and a hand that was not overly clean was clapped over his mouth.

"Not a sound, Rover, if you know when you are well off!" said a voice into his ear.

Despite this warning the lad would have yelled to his brothers, but he found this impossible. He had been attacked by Merrick and Shelley, and Cuffer stood nearby, ready with a stick, to crack him over the head should he show fight. The attack had come in the dark, the gas lamp and the lantern, having been extinguished when the party from the *Josephine* drew close.

Merrick had prepared himself for his nefarious work, and in a twinkling he had Dick's hands bound behind him and had a gag placed in the youth's mouth. Then he had the lad bound fast to a nearby tree.

In the meantime Tom and Sam were sleeping soundly. The two brothers lay each with a hand close to the other, and with caution Merrick and his party tied the two hands together. Then they tied the lads' feet, so that they could not run.

"What's the meaning of this?" cried Tom, struggling to rise, as did Sam.

"It means you are prisoners!" cried Tad Sobber, who had had small part in the operations, but who was ready to do all the "crowing" possible.

"Prisoners!" gasped Sam. "Where is Dick?" he added.

"Also a prisoner," said Tad, with a chuckle. "You thought you had fooled us nicely, but I guess we have turned the tables on you."

"I suspected you Rovers," said Sid Merrick.

"Really!" answered Tom, sarcastically. "You acted it!"

"See here, don't you get funny, young man. Please remember you are in our power."

"And we'll do some shooting, if we have to," added Tad, bombastically.

"Tad, I guess I can do the talking for this crowd," said his uncle.

"You were afraid of the ghosts, Tad," said Sam. "You must have run about a mile!" And the youngest Rover grinned in spite of the predicament he was in.

"You shut up I." roared Tad Sobber, and exhibited some of the brutality that had made him so hated at Putnam Hall by raising his foot and kicking Sam in the side.

"Stop!" cried the youngest Rover, in pain. "What a brute you are!"

"Leave my brother alone!" came from Tom.

"A fine coward you are, to kick him when he is a prisoner! You wouldn't dare to try it if he was free."

"I wouldn't, eh? I want you to understand I'm not afraid of anybody," blustered Tad. "I am—"

"Tad, be quiet," cried his uncle. "I am fully capable of managing this affair. Don't kick him again."

"Yes, but look here, Uncle Sid, they—"

"I will take care of things," cried Sid Merrick, and so sharply that his nephew at once subsided. But on the sly he shook his fist at both Tom and Sam.

"Maybe we had better make sure that nobody else is around," suggested Shelley, who had been Merrick's best aide in the capture.

"All right, look around if you want to," was Merrick's reply. "I am pretty certain these boys are alone here—although more persons from the steam yacht may be ashore."

They looked around, but, of course, found nobody else. Then Dick, Tom and Sam were tied in a row to three trees which were handy. Merrick took possession of their single weapon.

"I don't want you to hurt yourselves with it," he said, grimly.

"Merrick, this is a high handed proceeding," said Dick, when the gag was removed from his mouth.

"No more so than was your statement of owning the isle," was the answer.

"What are you going to do with us?"

"Nothing."

"I must say I don't understand you."

"What should I do with you? I don't enjoy your company. I am here solely to get that treasure, as you must know. I am going after that and leave you where you are."

"Bound to these trees?"

"Certainly."

"Supposing we can't get loose?" remonstrated Tom. "We may starve to death!"

"That will be your lookout. But I reckon you'll get loose sooner or later, although we've bound you pretty tight."

"Can I have a drink before you go?" asked Sam, who was dry.

"Don't give 'em a drop, Uncle Sid!" cried Tad. "They don't deserve it."

"Oh, they can have a drink," said Sid Merrick. "I'd give a drink even to a dog," he added, and passed around some water the boys had in a bottle.

Less than fifteen minutes later the three Rover boys found themselves alone in the forest. The Merrick party had lit their acetylene gas lamp and the lantern and struck out once more along the trail which they supposed would take them to the treasure cave. The boys heard them for a short distance, and then all became dark and silent around them.

"Well, now we are in a pickle and no mistake," remarked Sam, with a long sigh.

"That ghost business proved a boomerang," was Tom's comment. "It's a pity we didn't dig out for the shore, signal to the steam yacht, and tell father and the others about what was going on."

"There is no use crying over spilt milk," said Dick. "The first thing to do is to get free."

"Yes, and that's real easy," sniffed Tom. "I am bound up like a bale of hay to be shipped to the South Pole!"

"And the cord on my wrists is cutting right into the flesh," said Sam.

"If we were the heroes of a dime novel we'd shoo these ropes away in a jiffy," went on Tom, with a grin his brothers could not see. "But being plain, everyday American boys I'm afraid we'll have to stay tied up until somebody comes to cut us loose."

"Oh, for a faithful dog!" sighed Sam. "I saw a moving picture once in which a dog came and untied a girl who was fastened to a tree. I'd give as much as five dollars for that dog right now."

"Make it six and a half, Sam, and I'll go half," answered Tom.

"Well, this is no joke," declared Dick, almost severely. "We must get free somehow—or they'll get that treasure and be off with it before father and the others have a chance to land. We've got to do something."

They all agreed they "had to do something," but what that something was to be was not clear. They worked over their bonds until their wrists were cut and bleeding and then gave the task up. It was so dark they could see each other but dimly, and the darkness and quietness made them anything but lighthearted.

"Supposing some wild beast comes to chew us up," said Sam, presently, after a silence that was positively painful.

"We know there are no big beasts on these islands," answered Dick. "Don't worry yourself unnecessarily, Sam. We've got troubles enough as it is."

"The only beasts here are human beasts," said Tom, "and their names are Merrick, Sobber, Cuffer and Shelley," and he said this so dryly his brothers had to laugh.

Slowly the night wore away, each hour dragging more than that which preceded it. Two or three times the boys tried again to liberate themselves, but fared no better than before, indeed, Dick fared worse, for he came close to spraining his left wrist. The pain for a while was intense and it was all he could do to keep from crying out.

"I'd like to know what time it is," said Sam, when the first streak of dawn began to show among the trees.

"And I'd like to know if Merrick has found the treasure cave," added Dick.

"It will soon be morning," came from Tom, and he was right. The rising sun did not penetrate to where they stood, but it tipped the tops of the trees with gold and made it light enough for them to see each other quite plainly.

The boys were glad that day had come at last, for being prisoners in the light was not half as bad as in the dark. Each looked at the others rather curiously.

"Well, we are still here," said Tom laconically.

"Yes, and liable to stay here," added Sam.

"I wonder if father is getting ready to land," said Dick. "I suppose if he does he will come ashore where we did."

"Yes, but that is a good distance from here," was Sam's comment.

"Wonder if it would do us any good to yell?" said Tom.

"And bring Merrick and his gang down on us," said his younger brother.

"No, thank you."

"I don't believe they are around," said Dick. "I am going to try my lungs." And he began to yell with all the power of his vocal organs. Then Tom and Sam joined in, and they kept this up, off and on, for fully an hour.

"I am not only dry but hungry," said Tom. "Wish I had that lunch we brought along."

"Tad Sobber sneaked that away," said Dick. "If ever there was a fellow with a heart of stone he's the chap. Why, Dan Baxter in his worst days wasn't as bad as this young rascal."

Another hour went by and then Dick uttered an exclamation:

"Listen!"

"What did you hear?" asked his brothers.

"I thought I heard somebody calling!"

They strained their ears and from a great distance heard a cry, but what it was they could not make out.

"Let's call back," said Dick.

"It may do us harm," interposed Sam.

"We'll take the chance," said Tom, and started a loud cry, in which all joined. They waited patiently for an answer to come back. But for several minutes there was absolute silence. Then, to their surprise, a pistol shot sounded out.

"Hullo!" ejaculated Dick. "Something is up, I wonder what it is?"

CHAPTER XXIII.
WHAT WINGATE HAD TO TELL

After the departure of the Rover boys from the steam yacht Mr. Rover and Captain Barforth held a consultation, and it was decided that the search for the treasure cave should begin in earnest at daybreak.

"I do not think the boys will locate the cave in the coming darkness," said Anderson Rover. "But still it will do no harm to let them have a try at it."

"Mr. Rover, do you suppose those on board the *Josephine* have landed yet?" asked Fred, who was present.

"There is no telling for certain, Fred. But I should say not, since their steamer is nowhere in sight."

"I hope they do not come for some days," said Mrs. Stanhope. "For if they do, and you meet, I feel sure there will be serious trouble."

After that Anderson Rover had a long talk with Bahama Bill, and the old tar said he thought he could locate the cave without much trouble.

"O' course, the isle has changed since I was here last," said he. "Must have had a hurricane or something like that, to wash the beach and rake down some o' the trees. But I think I can find it as soon as I locate the trail leadin' that way. You know trails are great things. Why, when I was sailing on the *Jessie D.*, from the South Sea Islands, we landed on a place where there was a trail running to a volcano. We took to it, and the first thing we know we went down into that ere volcano about a thousand feet. It made my hair stand on end, I can tell ye! Four o' us went down, an' the others had to git ropes an' haul us up ag'in, an' it took half a day to do it."

"Vos you hurted much?" asked Hans.

"Not a scratch, my hearty, only it broke my pipe, one my brother gave me afore I sailed, an' one I wouldn't have taken a month's pay for," concluded Bahama Bill.

An hour later Songbird, who was on the deck of the steam yacht, composing poetry in the darkness of the night, saw the old tar coming toward him. Bahama Bill was groaning deeply.

"What's the matter?" asked the would be post.

"Oh, I'm a burnin' up on my inside!" answered the old tar, and gave a deep groan. "I want a doctor, I do!"

Seeing Bahama Bill was really sick, Songbird went to his assistance and called Mr. Rover. Then Captain Barforth was consulted and he gave the man some medicine.

"It's queer I took sick so quick," said Bahama Bill, an hour later, when he felt better.

"What did you eat and drink?" asked Anderson Rover.

"I ate a tongue sandwich—one o' them was handed around awhile ago. I put it in my bunk room when I got it and ate it on going to bed. It made me sick the minit I downed it."

"I ate one of those sandwiches and it didn't hurt me," said Fred.

"Yah, and I vos eat two of dem," put in Hans. "Da vos goot, doo!" and he smacked his lips.

"Perhaps you ate something earlier in the day that didn't agree with you," said Captain Barforth; and there the talk ended, and Bahama Bill retired once more.

Less than an hour later came a commotion on the steam yacht. Two men were evidently fighting and the voice of Bahama Bill was heard.

"I've caught ye!" he bellowed. "No, ye ain't goin' to git away nuther!" And then came a crash as some article of furniture was tipped over.

A rush was made by Mr. Rover, the boys and several others, and to the astonishment of all Bahama Bill was discovered on the deck locked arm in arm with Walt Wingate, who was doing his best to break away.

"Wingate, you rascal!" shouted Anderson Rover, and caught the deck hand by the collar.

"Let me go!" yelled the fellow, and struggled to free himself. He held a pistol in one hand and this went off, but the bullet merely cut the air. Then the weapon was taken from him.

"So you are still on board, eh?" roared Captain Barforth, when he confronted the man. "What have you to say for yourself?"

"I—er—I haven't done anything wrong," was Wingate's stubborn reply.

"Oh, no, of course not!"

"He came at me in my sleep," cried Bahama Bill. "He had something in a little white paper and he was trying to put it into my mouth when I woke up an' caught him. I think he was going to poison me!" And he leaped forward and caught the prisoner by the throat.

"Le—let up!" gasped the deck hand. "It—it's all a mis— mistake! I wasn't going to poi—poison anybody."

"Maybe he vos poison does sandwiches, doo," suggested Hans. "I mean dose dot made Bahama Pill sick."

"Like as not he did," growled the old tar. "He's a bad one, he is!" And he shook the deck hand as a dog shakes a rat.

"He is surely in league with Sid Merrick," said Anderson Rover. He faced Wait Wingate sternly. "Do you dare deny it?"

At first Wingate did deny it, but when threatened with severe punishment unless he told the whole truth, he confessed.

"I used to know Sid Merrick years ago," he said. "He used me for a tool, he did. When we met at Nassau he told me what he wanted done and I agreed to do it, for some money he gave me and for more that he promised me."

"And what did you agree to do?" asked Anderson Rover.

"I agreed to get a job as a deck hand if I could and then, on the sly, cripple the yacht so she couldn't reach Treasure Isle as quick as the *Josephine*—the steamer Merrick is on. Then I also promised to make Bahama Bill sick if possible, so he couldn't go ashore and show you where the cave was. I wasn't going to poison him. The stuff I used was given to me by Merrick, who bought it at a drug store in Nausau. He said it would make Bahama Bill sleepy dopy, he called it."

"Did he tell you what the stuff was?"

"No."

"Then it may be poison after all," said Captain Barforth. "You took a big risk in using it, not to say anything about the villainy of using anything."

"Oh, jest let me git at him, cap'n!" came from Bahama Bill, who was being held back by Fred and Songbird. "I'll show him wot I think o' sech a measly scoundrel!" And he shook his brawny fist at the prisoner.

"I'm sorry now I had anything to do with Merrick," went on Walt Wingate. "He always did lead me around by the nose."

"Well, he has led many others that way," answered Anderson Rover, remembering the freight robbers.

"I am willing to do anything I can to make matters right," went on Wingate.

"O' course you are, now you're caught," sneered Bahama Bill.

"Can you tell us if the *Josephine* was coming to this spot?" asked Captain Barforth.

"Is this the south side of the isle?"

"Yes."

"Well, Captain Sackwell said he knew of a landing place on the north side of Treasure Isle, and he was bound for that spot."

"The north side!" cried Anderson Rover. He looked at Captain Barforth.

"Can they have tricked us?" he asked.

"I never heard o' any landing on that side," said Bahama Bill. "But then I never visited the place but onct, as I told ye afore."

"Did the Spaniard Doranez know of the landing on the north side?" questioned Songbird.

"So he told Merrick," answered Wingate. "He said he was the one to speak of the isle first, for he had visited it half a dozen times during his voyages among the West Indies."

"Then they may be on the north side of the island now!" cried Fred.

After that Walt Wingate was questioned closely and he told all he knew about Merrick and his plans. He was very humble, and insisted upon it that he had meant to do no more than put Bahama Bill into a sound sleep.

"Well, you are a dangerous character," said Captain Barforth. "For the present I am going to keep you a prisoner," and a few minutes later he had Wingate handcuffed and placed under lock and key in a small storeroom. The deck hand did not like this, but he was thankful to escape a worse fate.

Anxious to know if the *Josephine* was anywhere in the vicinity of the isle, some of those on board the *Rainbow* ascended one of the masts and attempted to look across the land. But a hill shut off the view.

"We'll have to wait until morning," said Mr. Rover, and was about to go down to the deck when something attracted his attention. It was a strange shaft of light shooting up from along the trees in the center of Treasure Isle.

"A searchlight!" he cried. "Somebody is on shore, and it must be Merrick with his crowd." And this surmise was correct, as we already know.

CHAPTER XXIV.
A MISSING LANDMARK

The searchlight was watched with interest for fully quarter of an hour. It was, of course, visible only now and then, but from the shafts of light seen, those on the steam yacht were certain somebody was moving from the north side of the isle to the location of the treasure cave.

"We ought to head them off, if possible," declared Anderson Rover. "Should that be Merrick's crowd and they meet my sons there will surely be trouble!"

"Let us go ashore without delay!" said Songbird, who was sorry he had not accompanied the Rover boys.

"That's what I say!" added Fred. "We can take plenty of lights."

"I vos not von pit sleepy," declared Hans. "I go kvick, of you said so, Mr. Rofer."

"If yo' go, don't forgit Aleck!" pleaded the colored man.

"You shall go, Aleck," answered Mr. Rover, who knew he could depend upon the colored man in any emergency.

"I hope you find Dick, and Tom and Sam," said Dora. "It was foolish for them to go off alone."

"And don't let Merrick hurt anybody," pleaded Nellie.

It was quickly decided that the party to go ashore should be composed of Mr. Rover, Bahama Bill, Aleck, and the three boys. Nearly everybody went armed, and the party carried with them a small electric searchlight, run by a "pocket" battery, and two oil lanterns. They also took with them some provisions, and a pick, a shovel and a crowbar, for Bahama Bill said there might be some digging to do to get at the treasure.

Had it not been for the small searchlight it would have been next to impossible to find the opening through the reef during the night.

But the light was all that was needed, and they came through with little more than a shower of spray touching them. Bahama Bill and Mr. Rover rowed the boat and soon brought the craft to a point where they disembarked without difficulty.

"The boys did not land here," said Anderson Rover, after a look along the sandy shore for footprints. "But they must have come in somewhere around here."

"Let's call for them," suggested Songbird, and this was done, but no reply came back.

"They have started on the hunt for the cave, just as I supposed they would," said Mr. Rover.

"Den let us git aftah dem directly," said Aleck. "I feels like I could tramp all night widout half tryin'!"

Tying up the rowboat, and shouldering their tools and provisions, they set off along the shore of Horseshoe Bay, just as the three Rover boys had done. Bahama Bill led the way, with Mr. Rover beside him, carrying the electric light, which gave out fully as much light as did the acetylene gas lamp carried by Merrick.

"Here are some footprints!" cried Mr. Rover, after a short distance had been covered.

"Dem was made by our boys!" cried Aleck, after a minute examination. "I know dem shoes, fo' I has shined 'em many de time!"

"If they walked in that direction they took the wrong course," was Bahama Bill's comment. "Like as not they got turned around among the trees an' in the dark."

"We must locate the party with that strong light we saw from the yacht," said Mr. Rover. "Perhaps in doing that we'll come up to my sons."

Once on shore, the old tar said he remembered the locality well, and he did not hesitate in pushing forward, across the path taken by the three Rover boys, and then to a trail which the Rovers had missed. They had to climb a small hill, and here it was that Bahama Bill showed the first signs of perplexity.

"Queer!" he muttered, coming to a halt and gazing around. "Mighty queer!"

"What is queer?" questioned Anderson Rover.

"This looks changed to me. When I was here afore there was a rock yonder, an' the crowd placed a mark on it fer a guide as I told ye. Ain't no rock there now!" And he scratched his head as if he was afraid he was not seeing aright.

"When you were here was a good many years ago," said Songbird. "The rock may have tumbled down the hill. Let us look around."

This advice was followed, and after a long hunt a rock was found in a hollow. It had a peculiar mark cut upon it.

"That's it!" cried Bahama Bill, in delight. "I knew it must be around here somewhere—but what made that big rock tumble down?"

"Maybe somepody pushed him ofer," said Hans.

"Four men couldn't budge that rock," declared Fred.

"I believe an earthquake must have done it," came from Anderson Rover, and suddenly his face grew grave. "I trust no earthquake has disturbed the treasure cave," he added.

They pushed on, but scarcely had they covered a quarter of a mile when Bahama Bill called another halt. And well he might, for the trail they had been following came to an abrupt end in front of a pit several rods in diameter and twenty to thirty feet deep. The bottom of the pit was choked up with rocks, dead trees and brushwood.

"What now?" asked Mr. Rover, and his tone betrayed his uneasiness.

"This wasn't here afore," said the old tar, briefly. He was so "stumped" he could scarcely speak.

"You are sure?"

"Dead certain."

"Then this isle has undoubtedly been visited by an earthquake within the last few years."

"Thet's it, Mr. Rover."

"Maybe the trail can be picked up on the other side of the hole," came from Fred. "Let us walk around."

He and some of the others started to do so, but soon came to a place where walking became uncertain and dangerous. Song bird went into one hole up to his waist and poor Hans disappeared entirely.

"Hellup! hellup!" roared the German boy. "Bull me owid, somepody!"

Aleck was close at hand, and reaching down into the hole he got hold of Hans' hand. It was a hard pull, but presently Anderson Rover took hold, too, and between him and the colored man they got the German youth to the surface. Hans' face and clothing were covered with dust and dirt and he was scratched in several places,

"I dink I was goin' t'rough to Chiny!" he said. "You pet my life I vos careful after dis vere I valk, yah!"

"The earthquake seems to have left this part of the isle full of pits and holes," said Mr. Rover. "I hope my boys have managed to steer clear of the dangerous places."

They soon found they had to turn back, and now Bahama Bill frankly declared that he was "all at sea," as he put it.

"Every landmark I knew has been swept away," he said. "All I can say is, the cave is in that direction," and he pointed with his hand. "But it may be buried out o' sight now," he added, dismally.

There was nothing to do but to retrace their steps, and this they did as far as they were able.

They had covered about half the distance when they saw a shaft of light shoot around the treetops near them.

"There is that strange light!" cried Songbird.

"Let us find out what it is!" added Fred.

They tried to follow the light and in doing this became hopelessly lost in the jungle. Then one of the boys struck one of the oil lanterns on a rock and smashed it, thus doing away with that much of the illumination they carried.

"We must be careful," said Anderson Rover. "We are making no progress so far as the treasure is concerned. We had better try to find our way back to the shore, and try to find my sons." And this was agreed to by all.

But it was no easy matter to get back to the shore, and an hour later found them in a tangle of undergrowth. Aleck was ahead, accompanied by Fred and Songbird.

"Hark! I heah something!" cried the colored man, presently.

"Somebody is calling!" cried Songbird.

"Maybe it's Dick and the others!" added Fred.

They called in return and then they fired off a pistol. There was a brief silence and then came the call once more.

"Come on, dis way!" yelled Aleck, and plunged through the underbrush with the boys following.

He continued to call and at last made out the voices of Dick, Tom and Sam quite plainly.

"I'se found de boys!" cried the colored man in delight. "I'se found de boys!" And he plunged on again until he gained the clearing where the three lads were tied to the trees. With his pocketknife he cut their bonds.

"Good for you, Aleck!" cried Dick. "I am more than glad to see you!"

"And so am I," added Sam and Tom in a breath.

Then the others came up, and the Rover boys had to tell their story, to which the members of the second party listened with the keenest of interest.

CHAPTER XXV.
THE TRAIL THROUGH THE JUNGLE

"Sid Merrick is certainly in deadly earnest," was Mr. Rover's comment, after the boys had finished their tale. "He means to get hold of that treasure by hook or by crook, and he will stop at nothing to gain his end."

"We want to go after him and his gang," said Dick. "We ought not to lose a minute doing it."

"Can you walk, Dick?"

"I guess so, although being tied up made me rather stiff."

"I see your wrist is bleeding."

"Yes, and I tried pretty hard to free myself."

"And I tried, too," added Sam. "But I couldn't budge a single knot."

"We could not unknot the knots," added Tom, who was bound to have his joke.

It was now morning, for which all were thankful. The lights were put out, and the whole party partook of some of the provisions on hand.

"I believe Merrick would have left us to starve," said Sam. "He is the greatest rascal I ever knew!"

The Rover boys pointed out the direction Sid Merrick and his party had taken. Bahama Bill said that trail was new to him, and if it led to the treasure cave he did not know it.

"But I'll know the cave as soon as I see it—if it is still there," he added.

"Well, you won't see it if it isn't there," said Dick, grimly. "That earthquake may have changed the whole face of that portion of the isle."

The trail appeared to make a wide sweep to the westward, and led them over ground that was unusually rough. The trailing vines were everywhere and they had to brush away innumerable spider webs as they progressed. Once Songbird came upon some spiders larger than any he had yet seen and two crawled on his shoulder, causing him to yell in fright.

"What's the matter?" asked Dick.

"Spiders! Two were just going to bite me, but I got rid of 'em!"

"Don't be afraid, Songbird," came from Tom. "Why don't you study them and write a poem about them?"

"A poem about spiders! Ugh!" And Songbird's face showed his disgust.

"Der spider vos a pusy little animal," observed Hans. "He sphins his veb und attends strictly to business. I dink I make up some boetry apout him," and the German boy began:

"Der vos von lettle sphider
Vot lifed owid in der voot,
He made himself a leetle veb
Und said dot it vos goot."

"Hurrah, for Hans!" cried Tom. "He's the true poet of spiderdom!" and then he added: "Hans, we'll crown you poet laureate if you say so."

"I ton't von no crown," answered Hans, complacently. "I chust so vell vear mine cap alretty."

As the party progressed the way become more uncertain, and at last they reached the edge of a swamp, beyond which was some kind of a canebrake. They saw numerous footprints in the soft soil, and these led further still to the westward.

"Listen!" said Dick, presently, and held up his hand.

All did as requested and from a distance heard somebody calling to somebody else. Then came a reply in Sid Merrick's voice.

"Merrick is talking to Shelley," said Dick. "They have lost the right trail, too."

"Hang the luck!" they heard Shelley say.

"No path at all?"

"None," answered Sid Merrick.

"There is no path here either—it's a regular jungle," came from Cuffer, who was not far off.

"I'm all stuck up with the thorns," put in Tad Sobber. "I think we were foolish to come to such a spot as this."

"You can go back if you want to," answered his uncle, who was evidently out of patience. "Nobody is keeping you."

"I am not going back alone—I couldn't find the way," answered Tad.

"Then don't growl."

"I reckon we'll all have to go back and wait till that Spaniard can show us the way," said Shelley.

"That's well enough to say, Shelley. But supposing those Rovers come here in the meantime?"

"Those boys?"

"Yes, and their father, and the others on that steam yacht," went on Sid Merrick earnestly.

"They can't find the cave any quicker than we can—if Wingate did as he promised."

"But if he didn't? He's a good deal of a coward and perhaps he didn't have the nerve to dose Bahama Bill."

More talk followed, but as the men were now moving in another direction the Rovers and their companions made out little more of the conversation.

"What shall we do, confront them?" asked Sam of his parent.

"Not if they are going back to their ship," answered Mr. Rover. "We can watch them and see what they do."

At the end of half an hour they saw that the Merrick party had started for the north side of the isle. They waited in silence until all were well out of hearing.

"I am glad we are rid of them—at least for the time being," said Anderson Rover. "Now we can continue the treasure hunt in peace."

"But dem fellers will be suah to come back," interposed Aleck.

"I know that, Aleck, but they won't come back right away. Evidently they are returning to their vessel to get that Spaniard, Doranez."

"I'd like to have punched Merrick's head for tying me up," growled Tom.

"It will be punishment enough for him if we get the treasure," answered Mr. Rover.

"If we do."

"You are not ready to give up yet, are you, Tom?"

"Oh, no. But finding that treasure isn't going to be as easy as I thought."

"We ought to be able to find some trace of the cave pretty soon—the isle is so small. If the isle was large it would be a different matter."

They decided to advance, some of the party skirting the swamp in one direction and some in another. It was difficult work and they did not wonder that Merrick and his party had given up in disgust. Occasionally they had to wade in water up to their ankles and then climb through brushwood that was all but impassible. They tore their clothing more than once, and scratches were numerous.

The sun had been shining brightly, but now, as if to add to their misery, it went under some heavy clouds, casting a deep gloom over the jungle.

"We are goin' to have a storm," said Bahama Bill. "An' when it comes I reckon it will be a lively one. I remember onct, when I was on the island o' Cuby, we got a hurricane that come Putty nigh to sweepin' everything off the place. It took one tree up jest whar I was standin' an' carried it 'bout half a mile out into the ocean. Thet tree struck the foremast o' a brig at anchor an' cut it off clean as a whistle. Some o' the sailors thought the end o' the world was comin'."

"They certainly do have some heavy hurricanes down here," remarked Anderson Rover. "But let us hope we'll escape all such, even though we get a wetting," he added, as he felt a few drops of rain.

Soon it was raining steadily, and when they reached a spot clear of trees they got soaked to the skin. But as it was very warm they did not mind this.

"It's like taking a bath without troubling about undressing," said Tom, and this remark caused a smile.

They were now in a bunch once more, with Bahama Bill leading them. The old tar was looking sharply ahead and soon he gave a grunt of satisfaction.

"What is it?" asked Anderson Rover eagerly. "I know where I am now," was the reply.

"And unless that earthquake knocked it skyhigh thet cave ought to be right ahead o' us!"

CHAPTER XXVI.
A DISMAYING DISCOVERY

The announcement that the treasure cave must be just ahead of them filled the entire party with renewed energy, and regardless of the rain, which was now coming down heavily, they pushed on behind Bahama Bill in a close bunch, each eager to be the first to behold the sought for spot.

There was no longer any trail, and they had to pick their way over rough rocks and through brushwood and vines which were thick regardless of the fact that they had little or no rooting places.

"I guess we've got to earn that treasure if we get it," said Sam, as he paused to get his breath.

"It certainly looks that way," answered Dick, as he wiped the rain and perspiration from his face. "I wonder how much further we have to go?"

That question was answered almost immediately, for Bahama Bill, turning the corner of several extra large rocks, came to a halt with a grunt of dissatisfaction.

"Well, what now?" questioned Anderson Rover.

"It's gone!"

"What, the cave?" asked several.

"Yes—she's gone, swallowed up, busted!" answered the old tar. "Thet air earthquake done it an' no error," he went on. "It jest shook thet pile o' rock wot made the cave into a heap, and there's the heap."

Bahama Bill pointed in front of him, where a large quantity of rocks lay in a scattered mass, many of them ten and twenty tons in weight. At one point was what he said had been the entrance to the cave, but this was completely blocked by the stones.

"Vot's der madder, can't ve get in?" queried Hans, with a look of real concern on his honest face.

"That doesn't look like it," answered Fred. "Too bad, and after coming so far for this treasure, too!"

"We must get in there somehow!" cried Dick.

"Why can't we blow up the rocks with dynamite," suggested Tom.

"We can—but it will take time," said his father. He turned to Bahama Bill. "About how far into the cave was the treasure placed?"

"Oh, at least a hundred feet maybe two hundred."

Anderson Rover heaved a deep sigh, which was echoed by his sons. To get down into that mass of rocks a distance of from one to two hundred feet would surely be a herculean task, if not an impossible one. And then, too, there was a question whether or not the treasure had not dropped down through some hole in the bottom of the cave after the earthquake.

"I'll have to think this over," said Anderson Rover, after an examination of the rocks. "We'll have to try to locate the treasure and then see if we can raise enough dynamite to blow the rocks away. More than likely, if we undertake the task, it will take a long time—perhaps weeks and months."

"What, as long as that?" cried Sam, in dismay.

"Well, if the treasure is as valuable as reported it will be worth it," answered Dick.

"But in the meantime, what of Sid Merrick and his gang?" asked Tom. "More than likely they will make us seven kinds of trouble and do their best to get the treasure away from us."

"We shall have to protect ourselves as well at we can," said Mr. Rover.

After that it rained so hard they were forced to seek shelter under a thick bunch of palms. The rain continued for half an hour longer and then the sun came out strongly, and the jungle became steaming hot.

With Bahama Bill to guide them, they walked around what had been the top of the treasure cave. From some landmarks which had not been totally destroyed by the earthquake the old tar felt certain that there could be no mistake and that the treasure must be buried beneath them.

"But how far down you'll have to go to reach it I can't tell," he added. "It's like them ile well diggers—sometimes they strike ile near the top o' the ground, an' then ag'in they have to bore putty deep down. It's my hope ye won't have to roll away more'n two or three rocks to git into the hole an' put your hands on the boxes with the gold and jewels."

"If we only had to roll away two or three rocks I'd be for doing the rolling right now!" cried Tom.

"I'd like to see you roll a rock weighing ten or fifteen tons," observed Songbird. "You'd want about twenty horses to even start it."

Now that the first disappointment was over, the Rovers began to consider getting down into the cave from a purely practical point. They looked over all the big rocks with care, making a note of such as ought to be blasted away and of others that could be removed with the aid of a rope and pulleys.

"Let us see if we cannot gain the shore of the bay in a straight line from here," said Mr. Rover, after the examination of the ground had come to an end. "If we can it will make it so much easier to go back and forth from the steam yacht."

They had a compass with them, and leaving the vicinity of the shattered cave, struck out in a direct line for Horseshoe Bay. Much to their surprise they found an easy path, and came out on the sandy beach almost before they knew it.

"Well, I never!" cried Dick. "If we had known of this before, what a lot of trouble we might have saved ourselves."

"Well, we know it now," answered Tom. "And as we marked the path it will be an easy matter in the future to go back and forth from the cave to the bay."

It took them some time to get their boat, and it was almost nightfall before they reached the steam yacht. It can readily be imagined that the Stanhopes and Lanings awaited their coming with interest.

"What success, Dick?" cried Dora eagerly.

"Not so very much as yet," he answered, soberly, for he hated to disappoint the girl who was so dear to him. And then he told her of all that had happened. She shuddered when she found he had been a prisoner of Sid Merrick and his followers.

"Oh, Dick, I am so thankful you escaped," she cried, with tears in her eyes. "You must not get into such a situation again! Why, the whole treasure isn't worth it."

"But I want to get that money and the jewels for you, Dora."

"Yes, but I don't want money and jewels if—if you are—are going to get hurt," she answered, and her deep eyes looked him through and through.

"I'll be careful after this—but we are going to get the treasure, sure thing," he added, stoutly.

"I was afraid an earthquake might have played pranks with that cave," was Captain Barforth's comment. "An earthquake can shake down the top of a cave quicker than it can shake down anything else. It doesn't take much to do it."

The captain said he had a fair quantity of powder on board, to be used in the cannon for saluting and signalling. If they wanted dynamite, however, he'd have to run over to one of the big islands for it.

"And then we may have trouble getting it," he added. "We'd probably have to buy up the supply of some contractor who happened to have it on hand."

"I don't like to think of leaving the island while Merrick and his crowd are around," answered Anderson Rover.

On the following morning Mr. Rover and Captain Barforth went ashore, taking Dick, Tom and Sam along. The steam yacht was left in charge of Asa Carey, and the mate was told to remain close to the mouth of the reef and to send some of the others ashore armed if there came a signal of distress.

"We have enemies on this isle," said Captain Barforth. "And they may try to do us harm."

"I'll watch out," answered the mate, shortly. And then he turned away with a thoughtful look on his sour countenance. That there was something on his mind was evident.

The small boat was brought ashore at the point where the path led directly to the sunken cave. Although there was a lively breeze blowing, those landing did so without mishap. They had with them some tools for digging, and also a rock drill and some powder.

"It will do no harm to blast one or two of the rocks and see what is underneath," said Anderson Rover. "We may possibly be lucky enough to find some entrance into the cave, although I must confess I doubt it."

When they got to the vicinity of the shattered cave they found everything as they had left it. Even a pick Tom had forgotten remained undisturbed.

"Evidently the Merrick crowd has not yet found its way here," said Dick.

"We shall have to be on our guard when we go to blasting," answered his parent. "For the noise may bring that rascal and his gang here in a hurry."

And then all set to work with vigor to see if by some means they could not get down under the rocks and to the spot where the precious treasure had been deposited so many years before.

CHAPTER XXVII.
WHAT HAPPENED ON THE STEAM YACHT

About an hour after the Rovers and Captain Barforth had left the steam yacht Dora came from the forward deck looking much disturbed.

"What is the trouble?" asked her mother.

"Oh, not very much," she answered, for she did not wish to worry her parent. "Where is Fred?"

"I think he is at the stern, fishing with Hans and John."

"I want to see them," continued Dora, and hurried off.

She found the three chums at the stern. They had been fishing for some time and several fish lay on the deck near them.

"Hullo, Dora, want to try your luck?" asked Fred, pleasantly. "I'll fix you a line—and fix lines for Nellie and Grace, too, if they want them."

"I want to tell you boys something," said the girl, in almost a whisper, and not noticing what Fred had proposed. "I-I am afraid something is going to happen."

"What's that?" asked Songbird, and all three youths looked at Dora anxiously.

"I was just up near the bow of the boat, and I overheard Mr. Carey, the mate, talking to Mr. Bossermann, the assistant engineer. You know I don't like those men a bit."

"None of us do," said Fred.

"Didn't ve haf a quarrel mid both of dem," added Hans.

"They were so in earnest that they did not notice me," continued Dora. "I was going to walk away when I saw them, but then I overheard the name of Walt Wingate and I turned back to learn what they were saying about that bad man. It seems both the mate and the assistant engineer have been talking to Wingate, and Wingate has made them an offer."

"Does Wingate want his liberty?" questioned Fred.

"Yes, and he wants more—he wants the mate and the assistant engineer to help him to defeat Mr. Rover's plan to get the treasure. He told Mr. Carey and Mr. Bossermann that if they would aid him he was sure Sid Merrick would reward them handsomely."

"And what did Carey and Bossermann say to that?" asked Songbird eagerly.

"They said they'd like to talk it over with Sid Merrick."

"The scoundrels!" vociferated Fred. "Talk it over with Merrick! We ought to put 'em, both in irons!"

"I wanted to hear more, but they walked away and I was afraid to follow them," continued Dora. "I thought I had better tell you and perhaps you'd know what to do. I didn't want to worry mother or my aunt."

"We ought to let Captain Barforth know of this at once," said Songbird.

"Chust vot I say," said Hans. "Der better der quicker."

"How can you let him know?"

"One of us might row ashore," said Fred. "The others ought to stay behind to watch affairs."

"I'll go ashore," said Songbird promptly.

"You'll have to have one of the sailors row you."

"I know it. I can take Hollbrook, he's a pretty decent sort of chap and I know he can row well."

The fishing lines were wound up, and without delay Songbird presented himself to Asa Carey.

He and the others had agreed to say nothing to the mate about what Dora had over heard.

"Mr. Carey, I wish to go ashore," he said. "Can I have Hollbrook row me to the beach?"

"Go ashore?" growled the mate. "I didn't know anybody else was going."

"Well, I've just made up my mind to go. Can Hollbrook take me in one of the small boats?"

"Why didn't you go when Captain Barforth went?"

"I didn't think of it then."

"I don't know that I can spare Hollbrook," grumbled the mate. He was eyeing Songbird in a suspicious manner.

"He doesn't seem to be doing anything just now."

"Say, who is running this vessel, you or I?" cried Asa Carey.

"Captain Barforth is running her. But she is under charter to Mr. Rover, and Mr. Rover told me to use a small boat whenever I pleased," answered Songbird sharply. "If you refuse to let me have a boat say so."

"Oh, I—er—I didn't say that," stammered the mate. "If you want to go do so. But I don't know if Hollbrook can get you through the reef in safety or not."

"I'll risk it," said Songbird briefly and hurried below to prepare himself for the trip. Fred and Hans met him in his stateroom.

"I think Carey is suspicious," said Songbird. "Keep an eye on him, and if anything goes wrong shoot off the cannon or a gun. I'll do my best to find Mr. Rover and the captain and bring them back as quickly as possible."

In a few minutes Songbird and the sailor were over the side of the *Rainbow*. Hollbrook could pull a long, telling stroke, and under his guidance the craft soon shot through the opening in the reef and glided safely into the bay.

"I am glad to put foot on shore," said the sailor, as he leaped out on the sand.

"I want you to remain near the boat," said Songbird. "I want to see the captain and it is possible we may want to get back to the steam yacht in a hurry."

"Oh! All right, sir."

"While I am gone watch the *Rainbow* and if she should steam away any great distance call me."

"Why, I thought orders were for us to remain near the reef," cried Hollbrook.

"So they were, but Mr. Carey is in command now."

Leaving the sailor on the sand, Songbird hurried up the path which the Rovers and Captain Barforth had taken earlier in the day. He had covered less than half the distance to the shattered cave when he heard a shout from the beach. Then, from the water, came the sound of a shotgun.

"Something is wrong already!" he gasped, as he stopped running. "I wonder what it can be?"

He hesitated, not knowing whether to go forward or back. Then he set up a yell on his own accord.

"Captain Barforth! Mr. Rover! This way, quick!" he called at the top of his lungs.

At first no answer came back, but presently he heard Tom's shrill whistle, and then a cry from Sam and Dick. The three Rover boys came down the path pell mell, and their father and the captain were not far behind them.

"What's the trouble?" came simultaneously from Dick and Tom. Sam would have asked the question too, but he was out of breath.

"It's Asa Carey," answered Songbird. And then, as the others came up, he told what Dora had overheard.

"And that shot we heard?" questioned Captain Barforth.

"It told that there was trouble on board, but what I don't know."

"Let us get to the shore," said Dick. He was thinking of Dora and her mother and the Lanings.

As quickly as possible they dashed along to the sandy beach. Hollbrook was still calling for Songbird.

"The yacht is steaming away!" he announced. "She is standing to the eastward."

Captain Barforth gave a look and something like a groan escaped him. The *Rainbow* was a good mile away from where she had been stationed since reaching Treasure Isle.

"Can it be possible Carey and Bossermann are running away with the vessel?" asked Sam.

"That would be both mutiny and robbery," answered the captain. "I gave orders to Carey to leave her where she was, unless a heavy blow threatened to send her in—then he was to stand off until the blow was over."

"Do you know what I think?" came from Dick. "I think he is going to sail around to the other side of the isle. Probably he has an idea of consulting with Sid Merrick. Then, if Merrick's offer suits him, he will do all he can to prevent us from getting the treasure."

"You mean he and Bossermann will throw in their fortunes with Merrick?" asked Mr. Rover.

"Yes, and as many more on the steam yacht as Carey can win over. I believe Carey is a rascal and Bossermann is no better."

"Yes, but they are only two against over a dozen?" said Captain Barforth.

"No, three, for you must remember they have Wingate with them," put in Tom.

"That is true."

"Can't we get to the yacht somehow?" asked Sam. He was thinking of Grace and the other girls, and wondering what would become of them in case there was a fight on board.

"No, that is out of the question," answered Mr. Rover. "All we can do is to remain on the isle and wait developments. If they land we can fight them, but not before."

CHAPTER XXVIII.
A NEW MOVE OF THE ENEMY

"Something is up."

It was Fred who spoke, only a few minutes after Songbird and the sailor in charge of the rowboat had left the side of the steam yacht. He addressed Hans.

"Vot you vos see?" asked the German youth.

"Look!"

Hans looked and beheld Walt Wingate on the deck, in earnest conversation with the mate. The deck hand was not handcuffed as he had been a short while before, when tramping the forward deck for air, by Captain Barforth's permission.

"Carey must haf daken dem handguffs off," said the German youth. "I ton't like dot. Maype dot Vingate make troubles, hey?"

The boys watched, and presently saw Bossermann come up and join the pair. Then Bossermann went below to the engine room. Shortly after this the yacht began to get up steam.

"We're moving!" cried Dora, as she came to the boys, accompanied by Nellie and Grace. "Oh, what does it mean?"

"I don't know," answered Fred.

"Can't you find out, Fred?" asked Nellie. "I am sure the captain said nothing about sailing before he went ashore."

"I'll find out—if the mate will tell me," answered Fred.

He walked over to where the mate stood, close to the wheelhouse, giving directions to the pilot of the *Rainbow*.

"Mr. Carey, where are we bound?" he asked, respectfully.

"Oh, just going to take a little sail around, to test the engine," was the apparent indifferent answer.

"Is the engine out of order?"

"Not exactly, but I thought it best to test the shaft. The assistant engineer thinks it is weak."

This was apparently a fair enough answer and Fred bowed and walked away. Then he went down the ladder leading to the engine room. He met Frank Norton coming up. There was a look of concern on the head engineer's honest face.

"Mr. Norton, is there anything wrong with the engine or the shaft?" asked Fred.

"Nothing the matter. Why?"

"Mr. Carey said there was, and he is taking a cruise around to test them—so he says."

"I don't understand it, Garrison. Everything O.K."

"Are you in charge now?"

"No, this is my hour off. Bossermann is in charge. By the way, I see Powell went off after the others."

"Yes, and I wish the others were back," answered Fred. He hesitated a moment. "Mr. Norton, I believe you have been with Captain Barforth a long time and that you and he are old chums."

"That's right."

"Then I can trust you, can't I? It is something which concerns Captain Barforth and this vessel very much."

"Sure you can trust me."

Without hesitation, for he felt sure Norton was both honest and reliable, Fred told his story to the head engineer, who nodded many times during the recital.

"I see it," whispered Norton. "I suspected something was wrong. Carey and Bossermann are in some sort of a plot with this Wingate, who came on board solely to aid that Sid Merrick. I believe Carey is going off to meet Merrick and see if he can make a deal with him."

"That is what I think. How can we thwart him?"

"Better fire that gun, as a signal to those on shore, first of all. Then we'll see what the mate has to say."

Fred needed no urging and soon he brought up a shotgun from the cabin and discharged it—the signal heard by Songbird, as we already know. Scarcely had this been accomplished when Asa Carey rushed down upon him from the pilot house.

"Hi! what did you do that for?" roared the mate, in sudden anger.

"Just for fun," answered Fred, as coolly as he could, although his heart beat rapidly.

"For fun?"

"Yes. Haven't I a right to fire a gun if I want to?"

"I reckon that was some sort of a signal for those on shore."

"And supposing it was, what then, Mr. Carey?" Fred put the question boldly and looked the mate squarely in the eyes as he spoke.

"Why—er—it's most unusual. There was no need of a signal."

"I wanted them to know we were moving, that's all."

"Humph! There was no use of alarming them. We'll be back long before they want to come aboard again."

"In that case I'll have nothing more to say."

"Don't you believe it?"

"I'm bound to believe it, if you say so."

"Don't get impudent, young man!"

"I am not impudent, and you needn't get impudent either!" cried Fred, his anger rising. "You are in command here, but this boat is under charter and just now I represent the man who owns that charter. If you have got to cruise around to test the engine and shaft well and good, but if you are merely cruising around for the fun of it I say go back to where we came from—none of us want to do any cruising today."

At this plain speech the mate grew purple in the face. He raised his hand as if to strike the youth, but just then Aleck came on deck, carrying a pitcher of ice water in his hand.

"Stop dat! Don't yo' go fo' to hit dat boy!" cried the colored man. "If yo' do I'll fling dis watah pitcher at yo' head!"

"You shut up, you rascally nigger!" shouted the mate. "You have nothing to say here!"

"I'se got somet'ing to say if yo' hit Massa Fred," answered Aleck, and held the water pitcher as if ready to launch it at the mate's head.

There was a moment of excitement and several crowded around, but then the mate waved the crowd away.

"I shall report this to Captain Barforth as soon as he comes back," he said, and turning on his heel, he walked off. Fred went down into the cabin, and Aleck followed him. A few minutes later Norton joined the youth and the others, who had gathered to talk the matter over.

"We must be on the watch," said the chief engineer. "I am certain now that Carey is up to some game."

A long discussion followed, but nothing came of it. The steam yacht kept on its way and rounded the eastern point of Treasure Isle. Then it stood to the north westward.

"I hope he knows his course," said Norton, to the boys. "If he doesn't he stands a good chance of running us on some key or reef."

If the boys were excited, the girls and ladies were more so. Nobody knew exactly what to do, and each minute added to the general anxiety.

At last the vessel rounded another point of the isle and came in sight of the sea beyond. There in the distance was a steamer at rest on the waves, and Fred and Hans felt certain she must be the *Josephine*.

The two vessels were soon close together. As the *Rainbow* came up to the other craft, Walt Wingate went to the rail and shouted something through a megaphone which the mate loaned him. Immediately came back an answering cry, but the boys did not catch what was said.

"This is going pretty far," said Fred, to Frank Norton. "Don't you think I ought to step in and stop it?"

The chief engineer shrugged his shoulders.

"Carey is really in command and it might be called mutiny to do anything to stop him."

"But supposing he allows Wingate to go to that other ship."

"Well, if Wingate goes we'll be well rid of him."

"Of course that is true, but still—"

Fred did not finish for just then Asa Carey came up.

"I am going to visit that other steamer," he said, to the chief engineer. "I shall take that man Wingate along, and Bossermann is going, too. You can remain right here until I get back."

Norton nodded, but said nothing. The mate looked at Fred as if to say more, but then apparently changed his mind and hurried away. Soon a small boat was over the side and this was manned by the mate, Bossermann, Wingate and a sailor named Ulligan, a fellow noted for his laziness and untrustworthiness. Without delay the small boat set out for the *Josephine.*

"I don't like this at all," said Fred. "Those fellows mean mischief as sure as you are born!"

"I dink da vos hatch owid somedings mid dot Merrick," said Hans.

"Perhaps they are plotting to gain possession of this yacht," was Dora's comment. "They may bring over a crowd to take possession and make us prisoners!"

"If they try any game like that we'll fight," answered Fred.

"Dat's right!" cried Aleck. "We'll fight, an' fight mighty hard, too!"

"If only the Rovers were here," sighed Dora. "I am sure they would know exactly what to do."

"They may be having their own troubles on land," said Mrs. Stanhope. "Sid Merrick is a very bad man and will do all in his power to get that treasure in his possession."

CHAPTER XXIX.
THE HUNT FOR THE TREASURE

With the *Rainbow* steaming away from Horseshoe Bay, the Rovers and those with them on shore felt that a crisis had been reached. If it was true that Carey, Bossermann and Wingate contemplated joining Sid Merrick there was no telling what the enemy might not accomplish next.

"I have never liked Carey," observed Captain Barforth. "But I did not imagine he would take matters in his own hands in this fashion. I did not think he had the backbone."

"It's the thought of the treasure has done it," answered Anderson Rover. "Many a man's head is turned because of gold."

Those on the shore watched the steam yacht round the eastern point of the isle. Each heart sank as the vessel disappeared from view.

"Well, we can do nothing at present, but hope for the best," observed the captain. "We cannot think of chasing them in the rowboats."

"We might tramp across the isle and see where they go to," suggested Tom. "The *Josephine* must be over there somewhere."

"Yes, we can do that," answered Mr. Rover. "But it will be a rough journey."

"I have a better idea," came from Dick. "Father has his spyglass with him. Why not ascend that hill back of where the treasure cave is and then get up in the highest tree there? A fellow ought to be able to see all around from that height."

"Hurrah! just the thing!" exclaimed Sam. He did not relish the long tramp through the thorn bushes and tangle of vines.

Dick's idea was acceptable to all, and they set off without further delay. They took the path leading to the shattered cave, and then mounted the small hill Dick had mentioned. Close to the top stood a large tree.

"Let me go up!" exclaimed Tom, who could climb like a cat, and he started without delay.

"Look out that you don't break your neck!" cried his parent.

"I'll be careful," answered the fun-loving youth. "This just suits me!" he added, enthusiastically.

"Can't I go, too?" asked Sam.

"If you are careful," answered Mr. Rover, and up went the lad, right on the heels of his brother. It was rather difficult work getting from limb to limb, for some were wide apart, but the vines, which used the tree as a trellis, aided them greatly. Soon Tom was close to the top and Sam speedily joined him. Then each took his turn at looking through the spyglass.

"I see the *Rainbow!*" cried Tom. "She is headed for the north side of the isle."

"Yes, and yonder is another vessel," returned Sam, as he pointed the glass in the direction. "That must be the *Josephine.*" And then the two youths shouted the news to those below.

After that the boys watched the progress of the steam yacht with interest, keeping those below informed of all that was going on. They saw the *Rainbow* draw closer to the other vessel, and saw the small boat leave the steam yacht.

"Four men are rowing to the other vessel," announced Tom. "We can't make out who they are."

They saw the four men board the other vessel and disappear, presumably into the cabin. Then came a wait of over half an hour.

"This is getting tiresome," said Tom.

"You can go below if you want to," answered Dick, who had come up, followed by Songbird.

Tom descended to the ground and Sam followed him. They had just done this when there came a cry from Dick:

"Two boats are putting off from that other vessel! Each of them is filled with men!"

"Are they coming ashore or going to my yacht?" demanded Captain Barforth.

"They are heading for the yacht!"

"They intend to capture the *Rainbow*!" groaned Mr. Rover. "Oh, if only we were on board!"

In his anxiety to see what was being done, he climbed the tree and so did the captain. Then the others came up, the tree being large and strong even at the top and capable of holding a good weight.

"If those rascals try to take my vessel I'll have them all hung!" roared Captain Barforth, and trembled with rage. "Oh, if only I was on board!" And he clenched his fists.

"Look! look!" ejaculated Dick, who had the spyglass. "I think—yes, the *Rainbow* is moving!"

"Moving!" came from the others.

"Yes, and she is turning away from the other vessel and from those in the rowboats!"

"Let me see," said the captain and took the spyglass. "You are right, Dick. The *Rainbow* is running away from them!"

The news was true, the steam yacht was indeed running away from the *Josephine* and from those in the rowboats who had set out to take possession of her. It was a time of great excitement.

"The rowboats are getting close to the *Rainbow*," said Tom, who had taken the glass. "The yacht doesn't seem to have much steam up."

"Perhaps the fires were banked when Carey left," suggested the captain. "Maybe they were put out, so the vessel couldn't move."

The steam yacht was moving slowly and those in the two rowboats were making every effort to catch up to her. Then the black smoke began to pour from the funnel of the *Josephine*.

"The other vessel is getting up steam," said Mr. Rover. "She may catch the *Rainbow* even if those in the rowboats do not."

Closer and closer to the steam yacht drew the two rowboats, until it looked as if the *Rainbow* would surely be boarded by the enemy. Then of a sudden there came a cloud of smoke from the deck of the steam yacht, followed by a stream of sparks which went whizzing just over the rowboats. Then followed more sparks, and balls of fire, red, white and blue.

"What in the world are they doing?" murmured Captain Barforth.

"They are shooting off something, but it is not a gun or a cannon," answered Mr. Rover.

"Hurrah! I know what it is!" cried Tom "Good for Fred and Hans! Those are my fireworks—those I had left from the Fourth of July celebration. They are giving them a dose of rockets and Roman candles!"

This news was true, and as the rockets and Roman candles hit the rowboats and the occupants the latter stopped rowing and then began to back water in confusion. Soon the rowboats turned back and hastened to the side of the *Josephine*.

"That's what I call repelling boarders!" said Captain Barforth, grimly. "I only hope the fireworks hold out."

"It is now to be a race between the *Rainbow* and that other craft," observed Mr. Rover, and he was right. Inside of fifteen minutes both vessels were headed out to sea, and running at about the same rate of speed. Soon the haze over the water hid both craft from view.

"Well, one thing is certain," said Mr. Rover. "Our friends are alive to their danger and are going to do their best to get away from the enemy."

"And another thing is that we are left marooned on this isle," said the captain.

The party remained in the tree a while longer, and then, as there seemed nothing else to do, they descended to the ground.

"Well, we have one thing in our favor," was Dick's comment. "Sid Merrick and his crowd must be on the *Josephine*, or they wouldn't chase the *Rainbow*, and that being so they can't interrupt our treasure hunt, at least for the present."

"But if they capture our steam yacht how are we to get away from here, even if we do uncover the treasure?" said Sam.

"We'll get away somehow—and make it good and hot for them in the bargain," answered Tom, and his father nodded in approval.

With their thoughts on the *Rainbow* and those on board, the treasure hunters went back to the vicinity of the shattered cave. Nobody felt much like working, yet to remain idle made the time hang heavily on their hands.

"There is no use of our going to work in a haphazard fashion," were Mr. Rover's words. "We must first go over the ground carefully and plan out just what is best to do. Otherwise a good portion of our energies will be wasted."

This was sound advice and was followed out. They surveyed the whole vicinity with care, poking in among the rocks with long sticks, and turning over such as were loose and easily moved.

"This looks as if it was going to be a long winded job," was Sam's comment, and he heaved a sigh. "I thought we'd come here, march into the cave, and put our hands right on the gold and diamonds!"

Dick was a short distance away, poking into a hole with a stick. The stick was over eight feet long, but the end did not appear to touch anything.

"There is some kind of a hollow below here," he said to the others. "I think we ought to investigate and see how large it is."

The others agreed with him, and all set to work to pull aside half a dozen rocks which were in the way. They had to use all their strength and even then the largest of the stones refused to budge.

"Let us get a small tree and use it for a pry," suggested Mr. Rover.

They had an ax with them, and Tom cut down the tree and trimmed it. Then, resting the log on one stone, they inserted the end under the big rock and pressed down with all their might.

"She's coming!" shouted Sam, as the big stone commenced to move.

"Yes, and look at the opening underneath," added Dick. "It must surely be part of the cave!"

The sight of the big hole made all eager to know if it was really a portion of the shattered cave and they worked on the big rock with renewed energy. Twice it slipped back on them, but then they got a new purchase and over it went and rolled out of the way. Then all of the treasure hunters got on their hands and knees to gaze down into the hole.

"It must be part of the cave," said Mr. Rover.

"I'll climb down on the rope," said Tom. "Hurry up, I can't wait!"

"You be careful, Tom, or you'll get hurt," warned his father. But it must be confessed he was as eager as his son to learn whether or not they had discovered the treasure cave.

Tom went down, and Dick and Sam came after him. The bottom of the hole was rough. On one side was another opening, leading to what certainly looked like a cave of considerable extent.

"Drop down the lantern," called Dick, and Captain Barforth did so. With the lantern lit Dick crawled into the side opening and his brothers followed.

"This is certainly a cave," said Tom. "But whether it is the right one or not remains to be seen."

"It must be a part of the original cave, Tom," answered Dick. "Because it is in the spot covered by the other. But it may not be the part that contained the treasure."

They crawled around, over the rough rocks and fallen dirt. It was a dangerous proceeding, for they did not know but what some stones might fall at any moment and crush them.

Suddenly Tom and Sam uttered the single exclamation:

"Look!"

Dick looked and then he, too, gave a cry. From under the edge of a rock they saw one end of a heavy wooden chest. A part of the side was split away and through the hole they saw a quantity of gold money!

CHAPTER XXX.
HOMEWARD BOUND—CONCLUSION

"The, treasure!"

The boys uttered the cry together and it thrilled those at the top of the opening as nothing else could have done.

"What's that?" cried Mr. Rover.

"We have found one of the chests," answered Dick.

"And it's full of gold pieces!" added Sam and Tom in a breath.

"Then this is the treasure cave after all," said Captain Barforth. "I must say you are in luck."

"I'd like to go down and have a look," put in Songbird eagerly.

All wanted to look, and in the end they came down one after another by way of the rope. The rock on the chest was lifted away and the strong box was dragged forth into the light. Sure enough, it was filled with gold, just as Bahama Bill had said it would be.

"Bahama Bill said there were three chests," said Mr. Rover, after the excitement of finding so much wealth had somewhat subsided. "Do you see anything of the other two?"

"Not yet—but they must be somewhere near," answered his oldest son.

Regardless of the danger of falling rocks, they commenced to dig around where the chest had been uncovered. They soon found a second chest, which contained more gold in leather bags, and also a quantity of jewelry and precious stones. Then, when they were almost ready to give up work for the day, they discovered the third chest, smashed flat under two heavy rocks, with its contents of gold scattered in all directions.

"We'll have to blow up those rocks to get all that gold," said Sam.

"Don't do that," warned Captain Barforth. "If you do you may cave in the whole roof and then the gold may be gone forever."

It was then decided to bring down the log, and pry the rocks away, and late as it was this was done, and they scooped up the loose golden pieces and put them in their pockets.

"It's a fine lot o' money," was the comment of Hollbrook, the sailor. "Wish some o' it was mine."

"You shall be well paid for your work, Hollbrook," answered Mr. Rover.

"Only stick by us and help us to get this to safety."

"Oh, I'll stick by you," was the ready answer. "I've got no use for such scoundrels as Carey and Bossermann. I'm only livin' one life, and I'll live that honest like, God helpin' me."

Night was coming on when they got the treasure to the surface of the ground. They hunted around diligently until they were almost certain they had everything of value. Each was exhausted from his labors, but all were happy. The Rovers were particularly delighted.

"This will make the Lanings and the Stanhopes independent for life," said Dick, to his brothers.

"And they deserve it," returned Tom. "Won't they be glad when they hear the news!"

"Remember one thing," said Sam. "We haven't got the treasure from the isle yet, and we don't know how the *Rainbow* is faring. If those on the *Josephine* capture our steam yacht I don't know what we are going to do."

"Well, we won't give up the treasure, no matter what happens," said Dick, stoutly.

Mr. Rover calculated that the treasure was worth more than Bahama Bill had said. Roughly estimated it would foot up to over a hundred thousand dollars, and this figure did not take in some jewelry of quaint design with precious stones which were new to the treasure hunters.

"For all we know those stones may be worth another ten thousand or more," said Dick. "I can tell you, it's a great find and no mistake!"

It was decided to take the treasure down to the shore of Horseshoe Bay and there bury it directly behind the sandy beach.

"And we'll leave everything here as near as possible as we found it," said Anderson Rover. "Then, if Sid Merrick comes, he can look for the treasure to his heart's content," and he winked at his sons.

"Good!" cried Tom. "I hope he breaks his back working to move the rocks."

Night had settled over Treasure Isle by the time the shore was reached with the treasure, which was carried in one of the chests and in several bundles and numerous pockets. Men and boys were thoroughly fagged out, and they sat down under the trees to rest before starting to place their find underground again.

"We might as well wait till morning," said Tom. "I want to have a look at that gold and that jewelry by daylight."

"We can wait," said his father. "So long as none of our enemies return to this isle we shall be safe."

They ate what little provisions were left and washed down the scanty meal with what water was left in the bottles. So far they had been unable to find any springs on the isle.

"I believe the want of fresh water is what keeps the natives away," was Captain Barforth's comment, and it is probable that his surmise was correct.

"I see a light!" cried Songbird, when they were on the point of retiring. "It is out on the water."

He pointed, and soon all made out the lights of a vessel in the distance. Then, as the craft came closer, they saw a rocket shoot up in the air, followed by a Roman candle.

"It's the *Rainbow*!" shouted Dick. "That must be some sort of signal for us!"

"But where is the *Josephine*" asked Tom.

Nobody knew, and just then nobody cared. Captain Barforth ran down to the water's edge and prepared to launch one of the small boats.

"I am going out to my vessel," he said. "Hollbrook, come along. If everything is all right, we'll send two rockets up or fire the cannon twice. Then you had better bring the treasure on board without delay."

This was agreed to, and in a moment more the captain and his man were afloat and rowing toward the opening of the reef with all their might. Those left behind waited anxiously for what might follow.

"The steam yacht may be in the hands of the enemy," said Songbird, but he was mistaken, for quarter of an hour later up went two rockets into the air. Then the searchlight struck the water, and those on shore saw a rowboat put off and head for land.

"It's Bahama Bill and one of the sailors," cried Tom, a little later. And then he raised his voice as the rowboat shot into the bay. "This way, Bill, this way!"

Soon the rowboat struck the sand and Bahama Bill leaped out. His face was one broad smile.

"So ye got the treasure after all, did ye!" he cried. "I'm powerful glad on it, yes, sir! Now we'll fool that Merrick crowd good!"

"But what of them and of their vessel?" asked Anderson Rover anxiously.

"Broke down an' drifting out on the ocean," answered the old tar, and then he continued: "You know how they tried to board us—after Carey, Bossermann, that skunk o' a Wingate, an' Ulligan went to 'em. Well, fust we kept 'em off with fireworks and with a shotgun. We didn't have much steam up, but Frank Norton—bless his heart—worked like a beaver, and the boys, Fred and Hans, helped him. I went to steer an' by good luck kept off the rocks an' reefs. They came after us pell mell an' onct or twict we thought sure they had us, an' all o' us got pistols and cutlasses an' prepared to fight. The ladies an' the gals was most scared to death an' locked themselves in their staterooms. But we put some ile on the fire an' putty soon we had steam enough up to bust, an' then we walked right away from 'em. I reckon the captain o' the *Josephine* was mad, for he kept on a followin' us and onct he got putty close ag'in. But then came some sort o' an explosion from the other boat, an' we see a cloud o' steam rushin' up from below, and somebody jumped overboard. Then the steam blew away an' the engine stopped, an' we went on—an' left them away out in the ocean, fifteen or twenty miles from here. We calkerlated they'd follow us soon as they could make repairs, so we came on at full speed, to take you on board."

"Is everybody safe?" asked Dick.

"Yes. That Dutch boy burnt himself ag'in with a rocket, but it ain't much an' he don't care, for he said the rocket hit a chap named Sobber in the stomach and keeled him over."

"Good for Hans!" cried Sam. "That will give Tad Sobber something to remember him by!"

As quickly as it could be done, the treasure was transferred to the two rowboats, and the entire party set out for the steam yacht. They were careful in going through the opening in the reef, for nobody wanted to see either boat swamped and its precious contents lost. The passage was made in safety, the searchlight aiding them.

"Back again!" cried Dick, as he mounted to the deck.

"Oh, Dick, are you safe?" cried Dora, rushing to him.

"Yes, and we have the treasure!" he answered proudly.

"Oh, how glad I am everybody is safe!" put in Nellie.

"We are all glad," said Mrs. Stanhope. "The last forty eight hours have been so full of peril!"

Of course everybody has to tell his or her story, and for a long time there was a perfect babel of voices. Fred and Hans related how the steam yacht had been rescued from the clutches of the enemy, and how Frank Norton had taken command and prevented anything in the shape of a mutiny. The ladies and girls told of how they had been scared and how they had locked themselves up in a stateroom, as Bahama Bill had said. Then the Rover boys had to tell all about the finding of the great treasure.

"And just to think!" cried Tom. "It is worth more than we at first supposed!" And in his glee he hugged both Mrs. Stanhope and Mrs. Laning, and then hugged Nellie. Nellie herself was so excited she never even noticed it.

In the meantime, Captain Barforth was consulting with the chief engineer and learning some of the particulars of how the mate had acted and how the steam yacht had been chased by the tramp steamer.

"I trust I did what was proper, Captain Barforth," said Norton, anxiously. "I tried to use my best judgment. From what Miss Stanhope overheard of the talk between Mr. Carey and that scoundrel of a Wingate I felt Mr. Carey was not the proper man to trust."

"You did exactly right," said the captain, "and what has happened since proves it. If Carey and Bossermann try to kick up any fuss I'll tend to them."

Mr. Rover was called into the consultation, and it was decided to leave the vicinity of Treasure Isle at once, before the *Josephine* should put in an appearance. It was a cloudy night, so they had to run with care and at reduced speed. They kept a constant lookout for the other vessel, but failed to sight her.

"Carey and Bossermann, as well as Ulligan, will have to remain on board of her," said Captain Barforth. "Mr. Rover wants to get back to Philadelphia as soon as possible with the treasure, and she is under his charter. If they want to kick up a fuss later, why, they can do it, that's all."

"Homeward bound!" cried Sam, enthusiastically.

"And with the treasure safe on board!" added Tom. "It seems almost too good to be true."

"And the enemy left behind," put in Dick. "I hope they go back and hunt for the stuff," he went on, with a grin.

His wish was fulfilled, as they learned a long time later, through one of the sailors composing the crew of the *Josephine*. The tramp steamer tried all of the next day to locate the steam yacht and then Sid Merrick ordered the craft back to Treasure Isle. Here, Merrick, Tad Sobber, Carey, Bossermann and several others worked for nearly a week trying to unearth the treasure, but, of course, without success. Then they had a quarrel with the Spaniard, Doranez, who would not keep sober. They accused the man of taking them to the wrong place, and in the fight that followed three men were seriously wounded. Then all went aboard the steamer and set sail for Cuba. The very next day the *Josephine* was caught in a hurricane, one of the worst experienced in the West Indies for many years. It drove the tramp steamer on the rocks, and before she could be gotten off several big holes were pounded into her and she went down. The sailor who told the story said he got away with four other sailors in a rowboat, and after a fearful experience lasting two days was picked up by a steamer bound for Havana. He did not know what had become of the others on board and was of the opinion that the most of them, if not all, had been drowned.

Fortunately for those on the steam yacht, the *Rainbow* weathered the hurricane well. The craft did a lot of plunging and pitching, and the ladies and girls had to keep below, but that was all. After the hurricane the weather became unusually fine, and the trip back to Philadelphia proved a pleasant one. Arriving at the Quaker City, Mr. Rover had the treasure deposited in a strong box of a local Trust

Company, and later it was divided according to the terms of Mr. Stanhope's will. This put a goodly sum in the bank for Dora and her mother, and also large amounts to the credit of Mrs. Laning and Nellie and Grace. The entire expenses of the trip were paid out of the treasure, and Captain Barforth and his men were not forgotten for their services. Mrs. Stanhope wanted to reward the boys, but not one would listen to this.

"Well, you are very kind," she said, to all of them. "If at any time you are in trouble, come to me. I shall not forget you." She, however, insisted upon presenting Dick with a new watch and chain and diamond pin to replace those stolen from him by Cuffer and Shelley.

"Well, that winds up the treasure hunt," observed Tom, as the whole party were on their way home. "Now for the next move on the programme."

"The next move is to go to school once more," said Dick. And he was right, as we shall learn in the next volume of this series, to be entitled, "The Rover Boys at College; Or, The Right Road and the Wrong." In that volume we shall meet many of our old friends once more, and learn the details of a plot against fun-loving Tom which had a most unlooked for ending. We shall also meet Dora and her cousins again, and see how they acted when their boy friends were in deep trouble.

The home coming for the Rover boys was full of pleasure. Uncle Randolph and Aunt Martha were at the depot to meet them, and the aunt gave each the warmest kind of a hug and kiss, while the uncle shook hands over and over again. Nor were Anderson Rover and Aleck forgotten.

"Back again, and glad of it," said Tom, as he flung his cap into the air. "The West Indies are all right, but give me Valley Brook farm every time."

"So say we all of us," sung out Dick and Sam, and here we will once again bid our friends goodbye.